The Cottage at the End of the World

By Jenny Twist

Credits

Editor: Emily Eva Editing
http://emilyevaediting.weebly.com/

Cover Art: SHP

Photo of forest
Photo by <a
href="https://stocksnap.io/author/freenaturestock">Fr
ee Nature Stock</a> from <a
href="https://stocksnap.io">StockSnap</a>

Photo of cottage
https://es.dreamstime.com/publicdomainphotos_in
fo

"This is the way the world ends
Not with a bang but a whimper."
T S Eliot

"You find your family as you go
through life."
Jonathan Sharpe

Contents

The Cottage at the End of the World

1. Gary

When Gary was twelve his parents were killed.

They died simultaneously and (he hoped) instantaneously when an articulated lorry, out of control on the M25, suddenly jack-knifed, its back end slewing into the left hand lane and sweeping into the line of slow traffic, resulting in the mangling of half a dozen cars before it finally ground to a stop.

Many years later he found a photograph of the crash in library microfilm archives under the headline **Horror Crash on M25. Eleven dead, five seriously injured.** Underneath was a photograph depicting a tangle of crushed vehicles. Impossible to identify his parents' BMW in that unholy mess. Hard to imagine *anyone* had survived that carnage. Probably better not to.

He was at boarding school at the time and Mr Dale, the English master, called him into the Headmaster's study. Fortunately, the Headmaster himself was not present. The Headmaster was a tall, thin, cadaverous creature with a distressing resemblance to Nosferatu, one of Gary's childhood horrors. *(That moment when Nosferatu was climbing the stairs and all you could see was his shadow, the long-fingered hands stretched out before him, waiting to grasp his unsuspecting victim)*. He always wore his academic gown, like a black vampire cloak. In fact, his nickname amongst the boys was Dracula. Gary never saw him smile but. if he did, he was sure it would reveal elongated upper canines, stained with blood.

Mr Dale was different. He was big and friendly and somehow comfortable, like a friendly bear. He pulled out two chairs and, instead of sitting behind the desk with Gary in front, like a penitent, he waved him to one of the chairs and sat down on the other himself.

"Bad news, I'm afraid, old chap," he said, leaning forward and patting Gary on the shoulder. And Gary stared at him in disbelief as he imparted the news. How could his parents be dead? He had only seen them the previous weekend.

~*~

The funny thing was that now he had very little memory of his parents. His mother seemed to be always on her way out to somewhere important, immaculately dressed and made-up, more like a princess than a mother somehow. His memories of his father were even more vague. A large, dark presence, who came in and filled the house with a vague foreboding. If Gary hadn't seen photographs of him, he didn't think he would have any idea of what his father had looked like.

But he remembered Mr Dale, who was his favourite master. To be fair, he was everyone's favourite master. Not only was he a hundred times more entertaining than any of the others, telling jokes and acting out the parts in the books and plays, instead of just reading out pages of dull text or, worse still, making some unfortunate boy stand and read out his homework essay in order to have it dissected and mocked by the rest of the class.

Mr Dale used to quite often join a group of his students in the break and chat about all sorts of other stuff – not English. Stuff like football – he supported Manchester City – and the latest pop groups.

Gary had the impression Mr Dale was not as popular with the other masters as he was with the boys. For a start, a proper gentleman (and the whole point of the school was to produce gentlemen) would follow rugby, not soccer. That was a man's game. Soccer was for the plebs. Looking back, he thought Mr Dale had been the major influence in his life so far.

It was Mr Dale who instilled in him a love of reading. Mr Dale used to lend him books that weren't on the school curriculum, but were nevertheless well-written and exciting in a way most of those on the curriculum were not. Ray Bradbury, Robert Heinlein and Stephen King. "Just because a book is popular fiction, doesn't mean it's not literature, Gary," he had said.

Malcolm said his hero worship of Mr Dale was based on his need for a father figure, and Gary thought he was probably right. After all, his own father had not been much shakes as a father figure and hadn't even stuck around long enough to improve. Not that it was his fault. He realised that. Nobody *chose* to be crushed under an articulated lorry and turned into spaghetti sauce. But still . . .

Actually, his very friendship with Malcolm was probably down to Mr Dale's happy acceptance of people from all walks of life, being himself not quite from the usual run of master material.

Malcolm was a day boy, the son of a local farmer, who had been awarded a bursary for his outstanding results in the eleven plus and the school entrance exam. It paid the school fees, but it still didn't cover everything, Malcolm had confided in Gary, and his parents really struggled to pay for his uniform and books and so forth. His mother had got his entire uniform from the school second hand stall and consequently most of his clothes didn't quite fit and had clearly seen some considerable use before Malcolm stepped into them. Also, he had a local accent, which he made no attempt to hide.

All this added up to him being considered an upstart and a pleb by the rest of the boys. Malcolm accepted this cheerfully. "After all, I *am* a pleb," he said. "From the Latin – plebeian – one of the common people," he added helpfully. Malcolm liked Mr Dale because he was a pleb too.

Gary didn't care whether Mr Dale was a pleb. Mr Dale was, in his opinion, a perfect human being – kind, funny and clever. Gary wanted to be just like him when he grew up.

It was no doubt because Mr Dale was such a good teacher that Gary ended up doing an English degree. How often, he wondered, was the course of people's lives determined by one inspirational teacher?

He had imagined that once he had graduated, his real life would start. His legacy from his parents, from their savings and the sale of the (rather pretentious) house in Dorchester, had paid for the rest of his schooling and seen him through university without benefit of a student loan, leaving enough over for a hefty deposit on the tiny but horrendously expensive shoebox of an apartment in central London.

London in those days was a bustling city, full of traffic and people in a hurry, coming and going to jobs that were mostly unproductive and unnecessary but paid well. Estate agents, bankers, stockbrokers, accountants, lawyers, members of Parliament – people who thought they were important but were really just a drain on resources.

Gary himself was doing an entirely unnecessary job as a freelance journalist, writing articles on culture. He wasn't even doing meaningful work as an investigative journalist, working in a war zone or uncovering spy networks, just writing a load of mildly entertaining drivel about plays and novels and once, disastrously, on a fashion show. He couldn't find anything mildly entertaining to say about the skeletal girls parading the catwalk in clothes that cost thousands of pounds and couldn't possibly be worn in public except to a fancy dress party.

But his present job was just a stop gap – a way of earning enough money to support himself whilst he embarked on the illustrious career he had planned. Between reports on the latest happenings in the London theatre scene and art galleries he was writing his first novel – a cutting edge exposure of everything that was wrong with society. Mr Dale would be proud.

So it was with a light heart that he threaded his way through the evening crowds of office workers hurrying home and tourists making their way back to their hotels. He was heading towards a small art gallery near Trafalgar Square which was presently exhibiting a variety of obscure young artists. This evening it was hosting a small welcoming party for a few elite clients and, of course, the press.

And so it was without a thought other than a vague hope that he might find something truly original to write about, that he found himself suddenly catapulted into his real life. And it was not the one he was expecting at all.

2. Chloe

Chloe balanced precariously at the top of the ladder as Laura held it and shouted instructions from below.

"Bit more to the right."

Chloe swung dangerously to the right, feeling the ladder shift under her as she pushed the picture a little further along the wall.

"No, that's too much."

She moved the picture ever so carefully about half an inch left.

"Stop! Perfect. You're a star!"

Chloe gave a sigh of relief and climbed cautiously down. She didn't like ladders. Didn't like heights at all, for that matter. Especially if she wasn't protected somehow. She was fine if there was a wall or even a window between her and the drop. She didn't mind flying, for instance, but she couldn't go up iron staircases, like the ones on fire escapes. Even though, logically, she knew she couldn't fall through the narrow grating, just being able to see the ground below was terrifying.

It was a measure of how much she cared about Laura that she was here at all, never mind climbing bloody ladders.

She and Laura had grown up next door to each other on a housing estate in Yorkshire. Played together, went to school together, experimented with make-up and boys and smoking and alcohol. Shared secrets.

That was before Chloe's mother suddenly disappeared and was discovered a few days later, shacked up with a management consultant in Guildford.

Chloe could still hardly believe it had happened. Her mother had, up to that point, been a perfectly normal, reasonably happy, *respectable* person. She was a staff supervisor at their local Tesco branch and had been offered a store management position. Whether this went to her head, or whether she was suffering from some sort of mid-life crisis, Chloe had never quite sorted out. All she knew was that her mother went off to attend a week's training course in Manchester and never came home.

The family never suspected anything was wrong until she failed to arrive on the Friday seven pm train. At first they thought she'd missed it, or that maybe they'd misunderstood the letter describing the course, but her father couldn't find the letter to check, so perhaps she'd taken it with her.

When she still hadn't arrived by lunchtime the next day, Chloe, unable to stand the tense atmosphere in the house, had gone to the store where her mother worked and asked to speak to the manager. The girl on the checkout recognised her. "You're Vera's lass, aren't you?" she said. "Is there something wrong? She's not ill or anything, is she?"

At this, Chloe, to her intense embarrassment, burst into tears.

"Oh my God, something's happened, hasn't it?" The girl got up from behind the checkout desk and came to put her arm round Chloe's shoulder.

"I don't know," Chloe sobbed. "She never came home."

"Oh my God." The girl spoke into her microphone. "Can someone come and take over cashpoint four?"

A young woman with a ponytail came trotting down the aisle and slipped behind the desk. "What's up, love?" she asked, staring at the tear-stained Chloe. "Shoplifter?"

"No, it's Vera's lass. I just need to take her to the office."

The young woman watched, eyes bright with curiosity, as the cashier (Shirley, her name was Shirley, Chloe remembered) still with her arm around her, led her to the office. Behind her, there was a buzz of conversation and Chloe could feel the eyes staring at her back.

Sitting in the office, Shirley passed a box of tissues to Chloe, who blew her nose and then, using a different tissue, scrubbed fiercely at her eyes.

"Tell me what happened, Pet. Did your mum and dad have a row?"

Chloe shook her head. "No. Everything was just the same as normal, except she went on this training course in Manchester and she hasn't come back."

Shirley's eyes widened. "Not come back?"

The door opened and the manager stuck his head round it. "Everything all right, Miss Dobson?"

He eyed Chloe suspiciously. "Shoplifter?"

"No, Mr Banks, it's Vera's lass. She says her mother hasn't come home."

"But she wasn't working today –" Mr Banks began, then remembered. "She's on a training course. Hasn't she come back from the course?"

Chloe shook her head. "We don't know what happened. We don't even know the address of the hotel."

"It's not a hotel, it's a conference centre," Mr Banks muttered as he sat down behind his desk and ruffled through his inbox, finally producing a brochure, which he waved with a flourish, before running his finger down the first page and then picking up the phone.

"Hello, could I speak to the manager please?"

Chloe could only hear one side of the conversation.

"George Banks here, manager of Tesco, Selby branch. One of our trainees has not returned. Mrs Vera Silvers." Pause. "Friday? What time?" He glanced at Chloe, then half-turned away. "Yes, yes. I see. Do you have contact with this person." His shoulders hunched, he turned further away. "Yes, thank you. That would be very helpful. Yes please."

Mr Banks put the phone down and gave Chloe a dreadful, forced smile. More like a rictus than a smile. "It seems there's nothing to worry about, love.

She left with a friend. No doubt she's – um – just – er – visiting and will be back soon."

Chloe couldn't believe her ears. Her mother. *Her* mother. A woman of rigid respectability, who up to now had been a hard-working, dutiful wife and mother. A woman who had never in her life done anything unpredictable. *Her* mother had just gone off with someone she'd met at a conference and not even told anyone. And she had a horrible, sinking feeling that this unknown person was a man. It wasn't possible, surely?

She looked at Shirley, who didn't quite meet her eyes.

"My mum –" she began, and then realised she couldn't think of anything to say.

Mr Banks took his coat off the back of his chair. "Come on, love," he said. "Let's go and talk to your dad. Hold the fort, Shirley."

They went back to the house and Chloe listened behind the door as Mr Banks explained what had happened, confirming her worst fears. Well, not exactly her *worst* fears. Her worst fear was that her mother had been murdered.

Laura was as baffled as Chloe.

"Your mother?" she said. "I can't believe it. It's like being told the Queen has got a part-time job as a stripper."

Chloe's dad had not yet taken on board the concept of Women's Lib. It soon became clear that she was expected to take on all her mother's housewifely duties, as well as keeping up with her schoolwork. She had never realised before just how much her mother *did*. No wonder she ran off with a management consultant. This was nothing short of white slavery. She rang her mother, who was now in touch, but adamant that she wasn't coming home.

And that was how Chloe had ended up in Guildford, finishing her studies in a sixth form college. The management consultant bloke, Gordon, whom she had been prepared to hate, turned out to be a charming, funny and loving man. Under his care her mother blossomed into the attractive and delightful person she was meant to be, and they all lived happily ever after. Except her father, who went on grumbling and, after the divorce came through, went and married the barmaid in his local pub, who was nowhere near as biddable as her mother used to be.

When Laura went on to do a fine arts degree (in Manchester, ironically enough) Chloe joined her and did performing arts. Neither of them ran off with management consultants.

Now Chloe had a job in theatre design with a small London-based company. She wasn't earning quite enough to buy her own place, but Guildford was in easy commuting distance by train.

Her mother and Gordon had bought her a second-hand car for her 21st birthday and she had celebrated by driving up to Cumbria every couple of months to stay with Laura, who had taken up residence with her beloved Auntie Martha.

Auntie Martha's cottage was out in the middle of nowhere. In a wood, actually. A big wood. With pigs in it. And cottage was a misnomer. The house was massive. Laura had converted the large, south-facing conservatory into a studio and had been painting like a demon ever since.

When the London gallery had offered her the chance to exhibit, the first thing she had done was contact Chloe. And Chloe had dutifully taken two days off work to help. Yesterday she'd driven all the way to the cottage to help her parcel up the paintings and load them in the car – very carefully, with a blanket underneath them and another on top.

Laura was in a state of high excitement, fussing around, getting in the way. Her Auntie Martha had mostly just stood watching with an amused smile, every so often producing another cup of tea.

When the two girls had finally stowed the pictures to Laura's satisfaction, Auntie Martha had served up one of her famous beef cobblers, which Chloe ate with a kind of ravenous concentration but Laura picked at, too excited to eat properly.

The next morning – this morning – they'd driven to London, directly to the gallery, where a bored looking lout directed them to the carpark round the back, and then, despite being completely knackered from the long drive, Chloe had immediately been dragooned into helping hang the paintings.

Now they stood back to admire the fruits of their labour.

"Do you think maybe the thrush should be a little bit more to the—"

"No," Choe cut in decisively. "It's just perfect as it is. Let's go and find something to eat."

They left the lout to take the ladder away and went to the gallery café, which served quite a decent standard of food at a reasonable price (for London).

Well, it wasn't every day your best friend had her first exhibition.

3. The Exhibition

"It's a private exhibition tonight, sir."

The young man looked harassed. Perhaps Gary wasn't the first person to get past the front desk.

"Press," Gary said, flashing his invitation.

"Oh, right," the young man said. "But the reception doesn't start till 8 o'clock."

"I know," said Gary. "I wanted to take photographs before the crowds arrive."

"Oh, right." The young man looked discomforted. Maybe nobody had told him this might happen. He looked towards reception, where someone else was trying to get in. Someone else with a camera..

The young man gave a brief flap of his hand, as farewell and headed towards the newcomer.

Gary sighed. Oh, well, it wasn't a race. It was just that he liked to take in the atmosphere before other people spoilt it with their presence. Sticking his invitation back in his breast pocket, he moved into the main hall and briefly surveyed the exhibits. The walls were hung with paintings in clear blocks, each with a placard stating the artist's name. Between each block was a table of sculptures or pottery, also displaying a placard.

The nearest wall was dedicated to an Oxfordshire artist - mostly rural scenes in oils – riverbanks and woodlands. Just one depiction of the obligatory dreaming spires. But the one that caught his eye was of the towers of Didcot power station.

This had been part of the landscape of his youth. Dorchester was just down the road from Didcot, although a world away in terms of wealth and status. Gary had always rather liked the power station. Especially at night, when the towers were underlit and looked somehow both beautiful and sinister – like a scene from a dystopian future. They had blown up three of the towers a year ago. He had watched it on the news and nearly wept for the loss. The rest was scheduled for demolition in the next couple of years. They should have been preserved as part of our industrial heritage.

He took out his camera and took a series of shots. Another painting was of Wittenham Clumps, apart from the power station, the only break in the flat landscape for miles around. Two small hills, one of which boasted an iron age fort. He'd walked up there once to have a look but there was nothing much to see. He liked the name, though – Wittenham Clumps. It sounded like a statement to which the reply should be "Does it?"

The pictures were pleasant, but not particularly inspiring. Except for the power station, which would soon be gone forever. Part of his childhood lost. He was 23 years old and already he was seeing his childhood snatched away from him.

The table in between painting exhibits was full of pottery heads with holes in the top, which he found vaguely disturbing. It was only when he consulted the catalogue that he discovered they were plant pots. The accompanying photos showed some of the pots sprouting green, leafy hair. If anything, that was even more disturbing.

He dutifully took a couple of photos and moved on to the next wall, which was adorned with large, very bright abstracts. Gary had never really got his head round abstracts. He couldn't quite believe they meant anything. He stared for a while, trying to see what it was that the artist intended you to see. The only one that made any sense at all was one entitled 'Chaos'.

He photographed a couple, without much hope that he could say anything interesting about them at all.

Table number two was full of strange little stick figures in unlikely poses. Gary was beginning to wonder whether the youth of today had any imagination or, indeed talent, at all. Perhaps he was just too stupid to understand.

Then he turned the corner and stopped dead in his tracks.

This exhibition took up the whole of the wall. He was aware of a collection of smaller pictures at the sides but the wall was dominated by one huge abstract picture. At least, he thought it was abstract, but he wasn't sure. It seemed to have something. There was a message there if only he could grasp it.

A voice behind him said, "You're standing too close. Move back a bit."

He obediently took a step back.

"A bit more."

One more step and then suddenly everything fell into place. The picture was of butterflies. Dozens of them, all different colours and sizes. And he was seeing them in 3D. How could that be? Some of the wings were diaphanous and he could see through them to a dark green background. They even seemed to move. A slight flutter here and there at the edge of his vision. He gasped.

"Do you like it?" asked the voice.

For a moment he couldn't speak.

"It's . . . amazing," he finally managed to say. "How on earth is it done?"

"Mostly acrylics," said the voice. "Although I used some oils for the bush."

He could see now that the background was a tree with dark leaves and a sort of purple blossom - slightly out of focus, so the butterflies stood out in relief. He was subliminally aware that the voice must be the artist and that he should turn round and look at her. He was being discourteous.

But he couldn't drag his eyes away from the painting.

"How did you get the 3D effect?"

"I'm not sure I can explain," she said. "It's all a matter of angles. Some of the others are 3D as well," she added, "but I think the Buddleia works best."

Gary was confused, thinking at first she'd said 'Buddha' and he finally turned to look at her.

She couldn't be the artist, surely? She looked so young and so ordinary.

"Did you paint this?" He realised it sounded like an accusation. He could hear the disbelief in his own voice. And so could she. A tiny frown flickered across her face, but then she smiled. And all of a sudden she wasn't ordinary at all.

"Laura Kingsley," she said, holding out her hand.

"Gary Brent," he said as he shook it. "I'm a journalist. I'm writing a piece about the exhibition."

Laura looked pointedly at the camera dangling from his neck. "I thought you might be." And she laughed.

Gary had never been very comfortable with girls. He had no sisters or girl cousins and he'd spent his schooldays at a boys` boarding school. For years, the only women he knew had been a succession of aunts he had been dumped on during the holidays. He didn't know what to say to her.

"I-um, I suppose you did it from photographs."

"Not at all. They're all painted from life."

"But how did you get them to keep still?"

"I draw fast," she said. "And I have a good memory."

She paused. "And anyway they *do* stay still, for a while at least. That's a buddleia."

Gary frowned. "Which one?"

She laughed again. "Not one of the butterflies. It's a bush – a butterfly bush." Then, seeing his confusion (was she saying butterflies grew on trees?). "It attracts butterflies. Sometimes they hang around for ages. It's in my Auntie Martha's garden."

Their eyes locked and they both stopped talking. Gary found himself gazing into her eyes. And she was gazing back – serious now, searching his face.

Time spooled out between them.

Gary had never believed in love at first sight. *Lust* at first sight, yes, but love? The idea was ridiculous. And yet, here he was, trapped like a rabbit in the headlights. He was filled with euphoria. He wanted to take off his cloak and lay it down before her. He wanted to rescue her from dragons. She was a fairy tale princess, tall and willowy with hair the colour of honey – ethereal – like one of her butterflies. He was simultaneously euphoric and terrified - terrified that she would just walk away. Walk out of his life and into a different future.

Was that how it happened? Just like that? A smile?

The moment went on forever, or maybe just a few seconds. He had no way of telling. Then, abruptly, it was shattered.

"Laura. I was looking for you. I – oh, sorry. I didn't realise you were with someone."

Laura looked away and the strange contact was broken. He became aware of another girl standing beside them.

"Chloe. I was just coming to look for you."

Gary panicked. This was it. She was going away and he couldn't think what to say to stop her.

She turned back to him. "This is Chloe, my best friend."

She was tiny, like a pixie, with huge eyes and black hair in a short urchin cut. He had to bend down to speak to her.

With difficulty he found his voice. "Gary Brent," he said, extending his hand to the newcomer "I'm with the press." He winced. That sounded so pompous.

"Chloe has spent the last forty-eight hours driving up to Cumbria and back," said Laura. "She's absolutely knackered."

The earthy phrase almost made him laugh. Not so ethereal after all. And the girl did look tired. There were dark smudges under her eyes. But she smiled at him and said, "Pleased to meet you, Mr Brent. Chloe Silvers. Do you two know each other?"

Laura laughed. "No, we've only just met. I'm hoping Mr Brent will write something nice about my pictures." She winked at him. "I'll see you later. I ought to mingle."

Gary became aware that the gallery was beginning to fill up. He looked helplessly at Chloe. "Look," he said. "I've just got to take a few pictures before the crowds descend. Don't go away."

He had an idea that if he hung on to Chloe he wouldn't lose Laura.

Chloe stood obediently by his side as he snapped a dozen or so pictures of Laura's paintings, taking three of the butterfly picture.

"It's amazing, isn't it?" she murmured. "I don't know how she does it."

"Apparently it's all a matter of angles," he said, and Chloe laughed. "I've no idea whether the camera will be able to capture it."

Gary fiddled with his camera and brought up the pictures he'd taken so far, swiping through until he came to the butterflies. The first one was useless, just a jumble of shapes, but the other two looked more or less all right. But were they in 3D? Hard to tell without seeing them on a big screen.

"Let me see."

He passed her the camera and she studied the pictures.

"Do you think it's worked?" he asked.

"I can't tell," she said. "These two seem to be OK."

He took another three to be on the safe side, carefully standing at exactly the right distance.

A waiter came up to them offering a tray of champagne glasses. Gary took one but Chloe hesitated. "I shouldn't really. I'm driving."

But she took one anyway.

4. Auntie Martha

Martha woke up with the daylight, as she always did, pulled on her slippers and her dressing gown and went downstairs. She coaxed the fire back into life, put another log on top, checked the kettle to make sure there was enough water for a pot of tea, then put it on the hob over the hottest part of the fire.

The stove had been installed in the Victorian age and it still worked perfectly. In the 70 years she had lived in the cottage the only maintenance it had required was an occasional chimney clean. They built to last, the Victorians. None of your planned obsolescence rubbish. Like her. She had been built to last. At 92 years old she still had all her teeth (except one wisdom tooth she had had pulled when she was in her twenties) and the only concession she made to old age was to be careful not to carry anything too heavy. Five years ago she had suffered an alarming bout of sciatica and now she let up immediately at the warning signal of low back pain.

Bernie, who knew her routine, waited until she had straightened up and then came to her, tail wagging furiously, for his morning fuss. She let him out to do his business and then went to the privy to deal with her own.

The water bucket was nearly empty. She would ask Ben to refill it when he came round.

She went back into the house. The kettle was coming to the boil and she poured a little of the hot water into the teapot to warm it, swilled it round and emptied it in the sink, added tea leaves and filled it up with the rest of the boiling water. Leaving it on the side to brew, she fetched a tea cup down from the shelf.

Martha had been 21 years old when she moved into the cottage. It had been a godsend at the time – an inheritance from a great-aunt she hardly remembered. She had visited Great Aunt Grace once when she was a child, accompanied by her parents, who had been terribly disappointed and, in her father's case, outraged. There was a family belief that Great Aunt Grace was fabulously rich, but it was clear from the general air of shabbiness and dilapidation of the cottage that she was no better off than they were. Her father had fulminated (on the way home – not in front of Great Aunt Grace – even he was not quite that crass) that they had come all that way for nothing. The place was falling down. And why did she live in such an enormous house? It was disgusting – all that space for one person. It didn't look like it had received any attention for years. Probably the cast iron Victorian range was the newest addition.

But Martha had loved it. Great Aunt Grace had nine cats – *nine!* And six of them were little kittens. And she had a real live pony. The pony lived in its own little house at the back of the cottage, with an iron basket for his food and lots of straw on the floor for him to sleep on. He was called Albert, after a famous prince. The pony had his house and a whole forest to play in, and his only job was to pull a little cart (Great Aunt Grace called it a trap, confusingly) in which he took the Great Aunt to the village when she went shopping. Great Aunt Grace showed Martha the trap with the shafts for Albert to stand between and lots of leather straps and things.

"Come on," said Great Aunt Grace. "Let's harness him up and we'll go for a little ride."

And that's what they did, riding out of the yard and down to the village under the baffled and disapproving gaze of her parents.

They returned with some lovely cakes from the baker's shop, and Great Aunt Grace served high tea, while Martha played with the kittens. It was paradise. She couldn't understand why her parents didn't like it.

And then, years later, when she had almost forgotten Great Aunt Grace existed, out of the blue, she had died and left everything she owned to Martha. It turned out she had been fabulously rich after all. There was £30,000 in shares – an absolute fortune, more than her father could have earned in a lifetime.

"You can sell the house and spread the money round a bit," her father had said. And Martha, who up to then had never disobeyed her parents (not counting what happened with the soldier) had flatly refused. "Certainly not," she said. "I'm going to live there."

She did actually give them a thousand pounds, enough to pay off the mortgage on their own house, but that was as much as she was prepared to do. She had plans.

The cottage and the inheritance could not have come at a more providential moment. Three months before, she and her dearest friend, Violet, had been to a dance in the town hall. There had been some service men on leave and the girls, who at that time were working as land girls on a farm in the Dales, were ready to let their hair down. It was, as it turned out, the boys' last leave before the end of the war, although they didn't know it at the time. She and Violet, who had both been what they called 'lookers' in those days, had no difficulty in snaring the two most attractive of the soldiers, Colin and Rupert. They had left the party early, all of them more than a little tiddly on the fruit punch served by the vicar, who must have slipped something a bit stronger than fruit in the mix, and who would have been horrified if he had realised what it had led them to do. Even now Martha could hardly believe she had done it. Up to then she'd been a good girl. It was just . . . the punch and the warm evening – the secret safety of the woods – and Colin's woe-begone face as he told her he didn't want to die a virgin. And the noises coming from behind the nearby trees made it obvious that Violet and Rupert were indulging in the same thing, which seemed to make it all right somehow. Which just goes to show how wrong you can be.

By the time she realised she was up the duff, Colin had returned to the war and she was left wondering how the hell she was going to get out of this one. And then, out of the blue, she had been left the cottage. It was the perfect place to hide herself away. She bought a cheap wedding ring from Woolworths, moved into the cottage and told the people in the village that her husband was away fighting in the war.

Later she discovered that Colin had been killed in the D Day landings. Well, at least he didn't die a virgin. She hoped he had enjoyed his one and only sexual experience rather more than she had.

Violet's soldier did come home and Martha was their maid of honour. She wore a voluminous, empire line dress to conceal her condition, clutching the bridal bouquet in front of her, convinced everybody knew really. But no-one remarked on it and even her mother, who had a talent for ferreting out embarrassing secrets, seemed unaware. It was with relief that she returned to the safe haven of her cottage.

The cottage had been a farm once but it had been let to rack and ruin, and she went about restoring order.

Despite the enormous amount of money, she was careful with it, employing local men from the village to restore the building, and planting a vegetable garden so she could be self-sufficient. The rationing during the war had taught her what was actually important (food) and her experience as a land girl had taught her a lot about farming.

She decorated the smallest bedroom as a nursery. It was her one major extravagance. She bought a brand new cot and beautiful baby clothes and nursery furniture, placing all the tiny nighties and terry nappies, neatly folded, in the chest of drawers.

The old pony, Albert, was long gone and his successor, Dandy, seemed set on following him, refusing to come out of his stable and hardly eating at all. The trap was still there – standing lonely and abandoned in the shed next-door. There were chickens in the yard. They weren't fenced in but her lovely new neighbour, who had looked after them and the pony after the old lady died, assured her that they were safe from foxes. They always came home to roost at night and the door was too small for the foxes to get in.

The neighbour, who seemed too good to be true, had turned up the day she moved in, accompanied by a couple of border collies. "One of these is yours, if you want him, lass," he said. "He were Mrs Hathersage's but we took him back when she died. If you don't want him, I'll keep him. He's a good dog – very biddable and friendly."

"What's he called?" she had asked and he replied, "Bruno. All my dogs have names beginning with B. It's a family tradition."

"Let's see if he'll have me," she said, and bent down to stroke him.

She fed the chickens every day, rejoicing in collecting the eggs. *Fresh eggs every day!* An unheard of luxury after the deprivations of the war.

She turned her attention to the pony, who began to perk up when she spent time with him, grooming him and feeding him apples as well as his hay. Eventually, she would take him out with the trap again, but right now she needed something more substantial for what she had in mind.

She applied for her licence and bought a second-hand car of the kind her father referred to as a shooting-brake. (Heaven knows why. He'd never been shooting in his life.) What she liked about it was the whole back opened up and you could use it to transport furniture. In those days you didn't have to take a test. She was quite a competent driver anyway, having driven the farm vehicles during the war.

She got rid of the more appalling of the furnishings, some of which retained a distinct odour of cats, and replaced them with, mostly second-hand, comfortable sofas. Even if you were rich it wasn't that easy to get new stuff in the months after the war.

There were still a few cats in residence, half-feral, and she fed them and gave them what affection they were prepared to accept in memory of the wonderful Great Aunt Grace, who had rescued her.

She and the baby would have a good, comfortable life.

But then, after all her preparation, it turned out that there was no baby after all.

Martha had bought a book on pregnancy and baby care. It gave full descriptions of what to expect at each stage of the pregnancy and she had become concerned that, at five months, there had still been no movement from the baby. Those that she thought she had detected were so slight that she wondered whether it was the baby or just indigestion. Surely by now it should have been more definite?

So she went to see the doctor in the nearest village – Dr Jamieson. He was a pleasant, avuncular man who insisted on examining her without charge, since she was the widow of 'one of our brave soldiers'. She felt guilty about this but reasoned that, although she had never married Colin, the baby was undoubtedly his offspring and thus was entitled to special treatment.

But it turned out there was no baby. The baby had never existed except in her imagination. Dr Jamieson took her by the hand and explained, kindly, that she had what was known as a 'phantom pregnancy' brought about by a strong desire to bear a child. Mary Tudor, he said – Bloody Mary – had experienced the same phenomenon.

Martha didn't give a fig for Bloody Mary. From what little she remembered of Tudor history she hadn't been a very nice person anyway. But she cared about *her* baby. Her little girl (she had decided it was a girl). Her baby, who had her beautiful nursery waiting for her. Little Grace, who would have blonde hair and blue eyes and be perfect in every way. She had looked pleadingly at the doctor, hoping there was some mistake, but he shook his head. "I'm so sorry, Mrs Johnstone," he said. "It must be a great grief for you."

She had pressed her lips tightly together and stood up to go. She didn't trust herself to speak.

"It won't make any difference to your ability to have children," he said as she was leaving. And added, sadly, "One day,"

She nodded and left.

She left the nursery as it was and locked the door. Partly because she couldn't bear to look at it and partly because she thought, quite rightly as it turned out, that Violet would no doubt have children soon enough and when she came to visit, the nursery would have an occupant.

5. Gary

Gary woke up feeling cold and uncomfortable. He stretched and his arm knocked against something solid, but covered in a soft material. Alarmed, he opened his eyes. It took him a moment to realise he was looking at his own living room from an unfamiliar angle. He was lying on the floor. *What the . . .?*

There was something under the table. His iPod charger! He'd been looking for it for two days.

On reflection, he realised he wasn't directly on the floor, he was on some sort of mattress. He was, it seemed, on his sofa bed. It was one of those where the seat of the sofa could be unfolded and flopped out onto the floor. He'd never thought to test it out. But it wasn't bad, considering.

He'd assembled it himself. Had assembled all the furniture in his apartment, in fact, using flat packs from Ikea. It had taken him the best part of a month, laying out each piece of furniture carefully in exactly the same order as the illustration in the instructions, making sure he had every screw, hinge and knob, and painstakingly putting them together. He was proud of himself. He'd never attempted anything like that in his life before; he'd been completely useless in woodwork at school. Not much good at anything that required physical co-ordination, to be honest.

Malcolm, of course, would have assembled the lot before tea time without even consulting the instructions. Malcolm had a genius for understanding how things worked. He was good with his hands. Good at everything, in fact. He was on the rowing team and the cricket team and the rugby team (he'd had so many X-rays his family worried he'd never be able to father children). Won prizes for academic work. What they called an all-rounder.

They seemed ill-matched, Gary being a plodder and a swot, whereas Malcolm seemed to sail through life succeeding at everything with no apparent effort. Yet they had been the best of friends at school. Still were. Hadn't spoken to him for a few weeks, though. He made a mental note to catch up with him later today.

It took an effort to get off the sofa bed. In the end he rolled sideways off the mattress and crawled under the table to retrieve his charger. And, as if it had been a key to his subconscious, he suddenly remembered *why* he had spent the night on the sofa bed.

> *Laura!*
> *Oh my God!*
> He sat up and banged his head on the table.

~*~

Last night, at the gallery. Laura had wandered off to talk to one of the little groups of people standing about between the exhibitions and he had stayed glued to Chloe while he took the rest of the photos he needed for his article. To be on the safe side, he purloined a catalogue for reference. Chloe was still nursing her glass of champagne.

"Don't you like that?" he asked.

"Not much," she said, with a slight grimace. "I'm not keen on fizzy drinks."

Gary laughed. "Me neither. Let's go and see if they've got something more interesting at the bar."

The barman, who looked like an all-in wrestler in an evening suit, was stoically polishing glasses and setting them out on trays.

"Can I help you, sir?"

"We were just wondering whether you had anything other than champagne."

The waiter cocked his head towards the shelves at the back of the bar. They appeared to be stocked with every spirit under the sun. "And there's a selection of good wines."

Gary looked at Chloe. "What do you think?"

"Well, I quite like cocktails."

"Ah, there speaks a woman after my own heart." The waiter beamed at her in a manner Gary found faintly alarming. "I do a very nice tequila sunrise, and my piña colada is famous."

"Then I'd like the piña colada, please."

The barman looked pleased and began assembling ingredients. "The trick," he said, "is getting just the right balance. And how about you, sir?"

Gary scanned the bar top. "I don't suppose you have any beer."

The barman raised an eyebrow.

"Sorry, obviously not. Not that kind of occasion."

"Exactly so, sir. Perhaps a nice gin and tonic?"

"Lovely. Thank you."

Gary looked round the room. There was nowhere to sit down. Clearly you were supposed to stand around juggling a drink in one hand and a snack in the other. He could see waiters moving through the throng, bearing trays of vol-au-vents and other dainty morsels.

Chloe looked dead on her feet. He was worried about her.

He turned back to the barman.

"Is there anywhere we can sit? My friend is exhausted. She's been driving for two days."

The eyebrow went up again.

"We're here to support one of the artists, Laura Kingsley. Chloe drove up to Cumbria to fetch her, and back, of course."

"Laura Kingsley?" the barman asked. "The Butterfly girl?"

"That's the one." Gary was pleased the barman knew her.

"That's some picture, isn't it, sir? I've never seen anything like it before." And then, suddenly descending from his pomp. "You could have knocked me down with a feather. How the hell did she do it?"

"Apparently," Gary said, keeping an absolutely straight face, "it's all to do with angles."

He was aware of Chloe making a slight choking noise but daren't look at her.

"Well, it beats me," the barman said.

"This piña colada is absolutely delicious," Chloe said, smiling sweetly.

The barman smiled back.

"I tell you what, my lovely, you see that green door over there?" He waved towards the other end of the room. "You two go and have a sit down in there and I'll send you another couple of drinks in a little while."

He seemed to have suddenly turned into a benevolent uncle.

"Thank you so much." Was she actually fluttering her eyelashes?

Gary took her firmly by the arm and they walked off towards the enticing green door.

"All a matter of angles," muttered the barman. "Beats me."

"Isn't he wonderful?" Chloe whispered, as they headed for the green door. "Lovely face. I'd love to paint him."

Gary thought the barman had the face of a rather battered bulldog but he forbore to mention it, saying instead, "So you're an artist as well?"

"Sort of. Theatre design. But I'm a mere doodler compared with Laura. She's real genius."

"Yes," Gary said, and sighed, thinking there was no way she was going to look at him, a mere mortal.

Chloe grinned at him. "But she's a human being too."

How did women *do* that? He was sure he hadn't spoken the thought.

"Well, here we are," she said, stopping at the green door.

Gary was abruptly reminded of an ancient record beloved by one his ancient aunts – *There's an old piano and they play it hot behind the green door!*

But this green door concealed nothing more interesting than a couple of sofas and some coffee tables. Obviously, a staff common room.

"Oh, bliss!" said Chloe, sinking onto a sofa and throwing off her shoes. "My feet are killing me."

And she turned her attention to her piña colada. After an appreciative sip, she once again declared it delicious. "Knows his stuff, that barman."

Gary turned his attention to his camera, sifting through the photos, deciding what he could use and framing his article in his mind. He really should try to get it off to the paper before midnight if it was going to appear the next day but he didn't see how he could abandon Chloe. Nor did he want to leave without at least having a contact number for Laura. Well, actually he didn't want to leave without Laura. What he wanted to do was march back into the exhibition room, sweep her into his arms and carry her off bodily to his apartment.

"Have you got any idea when this – er – (What was it called? A soirée? A viewing?) "– this thing finishes?"

"Week on Saturday."

"No, I mean this evening."

Chloe looked at her watch. "I think she said ten o' clock. But it'll go on longer. These things always do."

Gary felt a mild panic. He didn't see how he could get back to his flat in time to write his piece.

"Oh God, I'm so tired."

Chloe drank the last of her piña colada in one gulp, placed her glass on a nearby table, lay down on the sofa and promptly went to sleep.

What now? He could hardly just leave her.

There was a discreet knock on the door. The waiter with more drinks?

"Come in."

It was Laura, a drink in each hand. "The barman sent me with these. Lovely man. Very complimentary. Wonderful face."

Then she noticed the sleeping Chloe. "Oh dear, I was afraid this would happen. I should have planned this better."

She joined Gary on the other sofa, passed him his gin and took a sip of Chloe's piña colada. "God, this is delicious. Not just a pretty face, that man."

"He looks like a bulldog." He said it without thinking.

"Yes, I know. Wonderful face. I wonder if I can get him to pose for me."

Baffled, Gary sipped at his own drink. He nodded toward the other sofa. "What are we going to do about Chloe? I don't think she's fit to drive. How far have you got to go?"

Laura chewed her lip. "Guildford. It's about twenty miles." Her face had a haunted look. "There's no way she's going to make it, is there?"

"Can't you get a taxi?"

Her expression changed to one of horror. "Have you any idea how much a taxi will cost to Guildford?"

Gary shook his head. He thought about offering to pay for it himself but, bearing in mind the parlous state of his finances at the moment, he held back. She was right. It would cost a fortune.

"A hotel?" he suggested tentatively.

She gave him a withering look. Then frowned.

"How about – " he began.

"Shush, I'm trying to think who I know who lives near here."

"You know me," said Gary.

He'd exchanged telephone numbers with Laura (Thank you, God) and written down his address. She looked at it dubiously.

"I have to go now," he said. "I have to write my article and get it in before midnight. Just give this to the driver. London cabbies are brilliant. They have 'the knowledge'." Then, seeing her blank look. "They won't give them their licence until they've passed an exam proving they know London inside-out, with the shortest routes between all points."

Laura was unconvinced but put the note carefully in her bag. She looked across at her sleeping friend.

"I'll take her now if you like. Then you can mingle to your heart's content until this thing is over."

"Would you?" She gave him the full force of her smile and he felt faint. "You are wonderful. I can't believe you're being so kind to us."

Gary couldn't believe she could be so naïve as to entrust her friend to a complete stranger. What if he'd been an axe murderer?

To his amazement, the article went like a dream. It just flowed. He read it through. It was perfect. Just the right professional tone. A nice, balanced review of the various exhibits. He'd winged it a bit with the abstracts – 'bold and inspiring with vigorous strokes and bright primary colours' – paraphrasing the description in the catalogue. The last paragraph read, "But for me, the star of the show was 'Buddleia' by Laura Kingsley. This magnificent work is a masterful *trompe-l'œil*. Stand back and the butterflies suddenly spring from the canvas in glorious 3D. You really need to see this in person. A photograph cannot convey the magical effect."

Had he overdone it? He didn't think so.

Frowning, he checked the text again, made a few corrections, attached his selection of photos, and clicked on send.

The doorbell buzzed and he picked up the phone. "Hello?"

"It's me, Laura." She sounded slightly nervous.

"Come on in. Push the door open when I buzz. I'll meet you at the top of the stairs."

He stood up, feeling every bit as nervous as he had on his first date (Malcolm's sister, Mary – what a disaster that had been).

Had Laura sounded nervous for the same reason? Or had she begun to have second thoughts along the lines of mass murderers?

But, when she came up the stairs, she didn't seem nervous at all.

"I wasn't sure it could be right. Just a door between shops," she said.

"Most apartments in the centre are like that. Ground level is at a premium for commercial properties."

When it came to apartments, of course, it was the penthouses that were at a premium. But, quite apart from considerations of expense, he had no desire to live on the top floor. A couple of months before he bought the flat there had been a horrendous fire in a London apartment block. People were trapped in their apartments and there was only one flight of stairs. Firefighters couldn't get to the higher floors because the stairs were blocked by people coming down. There were horrific reports of people throwing their babies down to the crowds below. Seventy-two people died.

So Gary had bought an apartment on the first floor in a building with two flights of stairs. Low enough to tie knotted sheets to the balcony rail and abseil down if necessary. Malcolm had laughed at him. "You are such a control freak, Gary. You don't just have a plan B; you have plans C and D."

Well, when both your parents were killed by an uncontrolled lorry, it made you do your level best to control those bits of your life that you could control.

He ushered Laura into the flat and she shrugged off her coat. "What a lovely flat!" she exclaimed. "Right in the centre of town!"

She walked across to the balcony window and looked out on the communal garden below. "Amazing! You are so lucky."

"Well, it's very small," Gary said apologetically. His aunt Delia had sniffed and said they were trying to put a quart into a pint pot. But he thought they'd done rather well to fit so much in to such a small footprint. You just had to be careful not to have too much furniture.

"No, it's lovely. A bijou residence." She strolled around, admiring everything. "Lovely furniture. Modern. Just right for the place. Minimal."

"I made them myself." He felt himself blushing. "Assembled them, I mean. The chairs and things. From Ikea."

"Brilliant!"

She paused expectantly. "What have you done with Sleeping Beauty?"

"She's in the bedroom. I changed the sheets and everything," he added hurriedly.

He led her to the bedroom door and she peeped in. Chloe lay in an untidy heap, on top of the covers, still fully-dressed.

"Where are you going to sleep?" Laura asked.

6. Ken and Dora

"I'm off now, Ken. Our Laura's in the paper."

For an appreciable few seconds Ken continued concentrating on his elaborate carving of a miniature refectory table before the sense of Dora's words seeped into his consciousness. By then the front door had slammed and Dora had rounded the corner and was out of sight.

What did she mean? And were the two sentences connected? Had she, for instance, gone to the paper shop to buy a copy of the paper Laura was in? Then he realised he was asking the wrong question. *Why* was Laura in the paper. He had an awful sinking feeling in his stomach as he tried to replay his wife's parting words. Had she sounded cheerful? Excited? Terrified? As far as he could recall she just sounded in a hurry. Surely if anything had happened to Laura she would have sounded different. Anything bad, that is.

He put down the model, grabbed his coat and ran after his wife.

~*~

Ken took up carving when he was in the merchant navy. Life on a merchant ship consisted mainly of periods of frantic activity interspersed with periods of unrelieved boredom. Most of the crew had some kind of hobby to keep them occupied. Ken chose carving.

He was also an avid collector. Over the years he had brought home artefacts, pictures and trophies from all over the world. Mainly Dora liked them, especially the dolls and fabrics. She loved the bright, colourful cottons and silks from Africa and Asia and used them as spreads and throw-overs. But she disapproved of some of Ken's trophies. There was a full zebra skin, for example, and an elephant's foot umbrella stand – not to mention the dozens of little ivory ornaments and those made from animal horns and antlers. All of these had been consigned to the third bedroom, known as Ken's Den.

He kept his woodworking and carving tools in there as well, now used exclusively for making tiny and exquisite dolls' house replicas. He had been offered good money for them but had never sold any of them, giving them instead to Laura when she was a child, and now saving them for Dora's hoped-for grandchildren. So far Laura had displayed no interest in providing these – hadn't, as far as he knew, even had a steady boyfriend.

"We're not getting any younger," Dora said. A statement which was so incontrovertibly true that he rarely responded.

Ken caught up with Dora before she reached the end of the street and grabbed her by the arm. "What do you mean, Laura's in the paper? What's happened?"

Dora looked surprised. "I told you," she said. "Don't you remember? She's got her first exhibition.

In London. It opens today. She called me this morning and said there's a piece about it in the Guardian. And she's got a mention." Dora beamed with pride.

Ken had a vague memory of her saying something about Laura having her paintings in a gallery but he hadn't really been paying attention.

"God, I'm sorry, love. You did tell me. I just thought it was a local thing, you know, in the village."

Dora smiled at him. "I probably told you when you were busy with your carving. You're dead to the world when you're carving. I should have known better. Come on, love, let's get to the paper shop and see what it says."

The morning papers were in racks outside the shop. Ken grabbed a copy of the Guardian and started flicking through.

"It'll be near the back," Dora said, looking over his shoulder. "They have a section on culture."

"Since when did you read the Guardian?" Ken said. "I thought you only bothered with the tabloids."

"Well, they're easier to read," Dora said. "I don't know why the others have to be so big. Do they think posh people have longer arms?"

"I wasn't having a go, love. I just thought that was what you read."

"Well, I changed my mind when they were all so nasty to Mr Corbyn. Seems to me he just wants to give people a decent life. Sheila told me the Guardian was much better. Not so biased. And she's right. I don't agree with all of it but at least it doesn't make me angry." After a moment's thought, she added. "And it's a sensible size as well."

Ken grinned at her. Political activism was the last thing he would have suspected in Dora. Perhaps he wasn't paying her enough attention. He had all the time in the world now he'd retired. Must try harder. He dutifully turned to the back pages.

"Here it is. Good God, look at this."

Exhibition Reveals Startling New Talent

He skimmed through the article until he saw his daughter's name.

"Listen - *But for me, the star of the show was 'Buddleia' by Laura Kingsley. This magnificent work is a masterful trompe-l'œil. Stand back and the butterflies suddenly spring from the canvas in glorious 3D. You really need to see this in person. A photograph cannot convey the magical effect.*" He paused for a moment, so proud of his daughter he could barely speak. Then he shook his head and repeated, "This magnificent work!"

"The star of the show!" Dora chipped in. "Our Laura. Oh, Ken, she's going to be famous." And she hugged him.

Mr Jenkins, the newsagent, appeared in the doorway. "Are you going to buy that paper, or do you think I'm a free library service?" But he smiled as he said it.

"It's our Laura, Mr Jenkins. She's in the paper." Dora was bursting with pride.

"Let me have a look."

Ken handed him the paper and pointed out the last paragraph.

"That's brilliant. Well done, Laura. Is this the picture?" He pointed to the photo of the Buddleia.

All three bent their heads over the page to study it.

"I can't say I can see it in 3D, can you?"

"I think I can – a bit," Dora said, doubtfully.

"But it says, look," said Ken. "*You really need to see this in person. A photograph cannot convey the magical effect.*"

Dora smiled at him. "Are you thinking what I'm thinking?"

He smiled back. "We'll get down there straight away."

He rolled the paper up, slipped it into his jacket, took Dora by the arm and turned towards the station.

"Hey! Are you going to buy that paper?"

Ken returned with a sheepish look.

"No, you're all right, lad. It's a present. I'm right proud of her myself,"

Mr Jenkins went back in the shop and started writing out a poster.

LOCAL ARTIST STAR OF LONDON EXHIBITION.

He whistled as he attached it to the Guardian stand.

"Oh, I don't know," Dora said when she saw the price of a return to London. "I had no idea it was so expensive to go by train. "Wouldn't it be better to get a bus?"

Ken was shocked himself – over two hundred pounds for the two of them return. That couldn't be right, surely?

"Let's go back home, pet. I've got an idea."

Ken sat at his computer – a new thing for him, but he was learning fast – and typed in 'Park and Ride London'.

Dora was upstairs titivating herself. She didn't want to let Laura down. Should she wear a hat? Or was that over the top? She decided instead to put some setting lotion on her hair and curl it with her hot air brush.

"Finchley Central!" Ken declared triumphantly. "Twenty-six minutes by tube to Charing Cross. Fare and parking twelve quid."

"I can't believe it," Dora said, as she settled herself in the car and fastened the seat belt. "I thought the government was supposed to be *encouraging* people to use public transport. It can't be right when it's two hundred quid to go by train and twelve quid to go by car."

Ken forbore to mention the cost of the petrol or the fact that you'd still have to pay for the tube if you had come by train. But she was right. There was a massive difference. But when had Dora become so concerned about the environment? He tried to remember whether she'd said anything like that last time he was on leave. Hadn't she bought a new waste bin with a section for compost?

She was right, anyway. He'd seen the plastic in the sea. Seen how much worse it had got recently. And he didn't like it either.

"And the last time I went on a train it was absolutely filthy and you couldn't get a seat."

He screened out Dora for the time being as he concentrated on finding the route to London. He hadn't had much experience of motorway driving. Mostly he only drove between Selby and Auntie Martha's cottage.

7. Gary and Laura

Gary put the coffee machine on and folded the sofa bed back in place while he waited for the coffee to percolate. Then he plugged his iPad into its charger (result!), sat at his desk and checked that the paper had published the article. Yes, there it was, under 'Culture'. There were already a dozen or so comments.

Both girls suddenly appeared at the bedroom door. They were each wearing one of Gary's tee shirts. Laura was in his favourite, the one with the picture of an alien on the front and the legend 'Take me to your dealer.' He privately resolved never to wash it again.

"Good morning!" The pair of them looked as fresh as daisies.

"Is that coffee I smell?"

"Sure, help yourself."

Laura headed for the kitchen but Chloe came and stood beside him. "Thank you," she said. "It was very good of you to put us up last night. And in your own bed, too."

She looked round the room. The sofa bed was now a sofa again, but his bedding and sleeping bag were in a heap on the floor. "Did you sleep on the floor?" she said.

He smiled at her. "No, it's a sofa bed. I made it myself." He'd have to stop saying that. It made him sound like a complete moron. "Assembled, I mean."

Laura's voice came from the kitchen. "How do you like your coffee?"

"Black, no sugar," he called back. "The article's in the Guardian, by the way."

"Oh wow!" She came bouncing back in, the tee shirt riding up perilously near her nether parts. "Let me see."

She leant over him and he could feel her breasts pressing against his back. He was having difficulty breathing.

"Wow!"

Laura skip-read down the page until she got to the last paragraph.

"Oh, Gary, that's lovely. What a lovely thing to say! You are totally fabulous!" And she kissed him. On the cheek. *She kissed him on the cheek!*

"I must ring my mum. She'll be well pleased."

"Where's the coffee?" said Chloe.

By the time they had eaten breakfast – toast and cereal – and had all showered and dressed, it was nearly lunchtime. The only food in the fridge was a piece of cheese and they'd eaten all the bread for breakfast, so they took their time walking to the gallery and stopped for lunch on the way.

"I don't suppose there'll be much going on yet, anyway," Gary said.

By the time they got to the gallery they had dawdled so much on the way that it was well into the afternoon and a considerable number of people were wandering around the Young Artists Exhibition. Gary grabbed both the girls by the hand, afraid he might lose them in the crowd. The main focus seemed to be at Laura's end of the room, where a whole bunch of people had gathered in front of the 'Buddleia' picture.

Laura gave a little cry and broke away, running towards a smartly-dressed couple standing directly in front of the picture, gazing at it.

"Mum! Dad!"

Oh shit! Her parents were here.

Gary felt a sudden shock of fear. And something else. Jealousy.

Laura ran straight to her mother's arms. They hugged each other, Laura's parents smiling with love and pride. All of them so pleased with each other.

Gary's parents had never hugged him like that. Or at least, if they did, he didn't remember. And he didn't feel much in the way of family love for them either. Maybe there was something wrong with him. And yet, if Mr Dale had been his father, something he used to fantasise about even before his parents were killed, he felt sure he would have loved him. And, although none of his aunts had been particularly affectionate, he had had brief experiences of motherlove when he'd visited Malcolm's family. Mrs Abrams had, quite literally, welcomed him with open arms and enveloped him in a massive bear hug. She fussed over him whenever he visited and, convinced they weren't feeding him properly at 'that school', had always sent him back with a food parcel. They may not have had much money, the Abrams, but they were very generous people.

Chloe squeezed his hand and smiled up at him.

"Don't worry. Ken and Dora are really nice. You'll like them."

And she led him towards the little family group at a rather more sedate pace than that just taken by Laura.

And it was all right. Everything was all right. He did like Ken and Dora, and they liked him. They complimented him on his 'wonderful' article. Ken gave him a hearty handshake and Dora kissed him on the cheek. He suspected that if he had been visiting them in their home she would have given him a food parcel.

Later, after Dora and Ken had left, Chloe went to her car and fetched a small suitcase back. "Here you are," she said, handing it over to Laura. "I'll come back on Friday to drive you back to the cottage."

"Thank you, darling," Laura said.

Had he offered to let her stay at the flat? He was so confused by the whirlpool of his feelings in the last twenty-four hours that he couldn't be certain. It looked like a set-up. On the other hand, it was exactly what he wanted – Laura to himself for a week. She was smiling at him again.

They walked back to the apartment, Laura insisting they stop at a baker's to buy bread for tomorrow's breakfast. "And what about dinner?" she said. "What's your favourite meal? I can cook most things."

"I can eat most things," Gary said.

They had spaghetti Bolognese with a nice bottle of Chardonnay.

Then they watched a film on television, sitting together on the sofa. Gary stretched his arm along the back of the sofa, his hand brushing Laura's hair. He could hardly breathe. Did she want him to kiss her? If he did, would she think he was being fresh. If he didn't would she think he didn't like her? What if she wanted sex? He went hot at the thought.

When the film had finished (later Gary had no recollection of what the film was about) they drank the rest of the wine, Laura doing most of the talking, telling him about her life, her family, the cottage in Cumbria. Gary looked at their empty glasses.

"I've no more wine, I'm afraid. I don't keep it in. But I've got beer. Or I could do a G and T. Oh, and I think I've got a bottle of Baileys."

Laura gave him a quizzical look.

"My aunt Delia. She sometimes drops in when she's in town." He gave a slight shudder. "She likes Baileys."

"I think I'll stick to the G and T," said Laura.

Eventually Laura stood and stretched. "Time for bed. It's been a long couple of days." She turned and headed for the bathroom. Then, pausing and looking over her shoulder. "Where are you going to sleep?"

The bed was much more comfortable than the sofa. He went to sleep spooning Laura and feeling happier than he had ever felt in his whole life before.

Laura was fast asleep, her chest rising and falling steadily. "I love you," he whispered. She turned towards him and smiled. "I know," she said.

~*~

Monday morning they ate the last of the bread for breakfast and were driven out of the flat by hunger.

"Got your phone?" he asked, as he unlocked the door.

"Oh," she said, rummaging in her bag. "Here it is." She switched it on. Nothing. "Oh dear. The battery's flat. Does it matter?"

"It's just – I don't know – I wanted to make sure we were in touch in case we got separated."

She laughed at him. "You do worry about stuff."

But she dutifully searched for the charger in her suitcase and plugged in the phone.

"We'll just have to hold hands," she said.

They went to their favourite baker's again and bought more crusty bread and a baguette and Laura insisted on buying something she called a 'vanilla slice' and he called a '*mille-feuille*'. "It's

French," he explained helpfully. "It means 'a thousand leaves."

In the butcher's she asked him whether he liked Jägerschnitzel.

"What is it?"

"Veal in a mushroom, cream and wine sauce."

"I like it," he said.

They got back to the flat and Laura set about assembling the ingredients. Gary hovered around her, passing her things, occasionally putting his arms around her and nuzzling her neck.

"Stop it," she said. "I can't concentrate."

He left her to it and went to check his emails.

"Oh, bloody hell."

"What? What is it?" Laura came out of the kitchen, dusting flour from her hands.

"It's the Guardian. They want me to do a follow-up on the article. It seems your butterflies have caused quite a stir."

"Let me see." She grabbed his phone and read rapidly down the screen. "Oh my God! I don't believe it. It says here the gallery has been packed out with visitors, all coming to see the Buddleia."

She looked at him, her eyes wide.

He laughed.

"It also asks if there's any possibility of tracking you down and doing an exclusive. Apparently the gallery can't find you."

"Oops."

She ran over to the shelf where her phone was on charge.

"Jesus. Five messages from the gallery. How embarrassing! All asking to see me."

"Tell them you'll call in this afternoon. Let's have lunch first."

He called the Guardian while Laura was in the kitchen.

"I'm really sorry. I've been out of circulation for a couple of days. I'm going to the gallery this afternoon. I can take more pictures and have the follow-up article to you this evening. Yes, yes, of course I can. Yes, I'm in touch with her. I'm sure she'll be only too happy."

He went into the kitchen and stood watching as Laura prepared lunch with practised, neat movements.

"I've called the paper," he said. She looked up and smiled. "They want an article straight away about the reaction to your pictures, and then they're wondering whether I can do a further article about you and your work. Maybe visit you in your studio. What do you think?"

"I think that would suit me perfectly," she said.

~*~

Mr Dickinson was a small, round man with an almost bald head and bushy tufts of hair above his ears. For some reason this gave him the appearance of a small, furry mammal – a vole, perhaps.

"Miss Kingsley," he said, standing and shaking her hand, "So good of you to come in." Was there a trace of sarcasm there? No, she thought not. He seemed genuinely enthused.

"Sorry I didn't respond more quickly,·" Laura said. "I've been having trouble with my phone." Not entirely a lie. She had been too wrapped-up in her feelings for Gary to even remember she had a phone. "And this is my friend, Mr Brent."

Mr Dickinson peered at Gary over the top of his rimless glasses which, rather oddly, enhanced his resemblance to a vole.

"Pleased to meet you, Mr – er – Brent."

They all sat down and Mr Dickinson leant forward, his hands steepled under his chin.

"I have some very good news for you, Miss Kingsley. We have sold every single one of your paintings." Then, seeing her stricken expression, he added hurriedly, "Except the Buddleia, of course, which you reserved."

Gary gave her a questioning look but she frowned with a 'not now' gesture of her right hand.

"You will find your bank account considerably enhanced."

He beamed like a benevolent uncle – or vole.

"I don't know what to say," Laura said.

"It seems there was an article in the Guardian, which aroused considerable interest. I contacted the paper to let them know and they said they'd contact the journalist who wrote it to see whether he could do a follow-up piece."

Gary blushed deeply. "Sorry about that, Sir. I've been out of circulation for a couple of days." Laura made a small choking noise, which he ignored. "I'll get cracking on it today."

"Good Lord," said Mr Dickinson. "You are the journalist? I assumed . . ." his voice tailed off, perhaps afraid he might make an indiscreet suggestion. "Well – er – the paper thought maybe a personal interview with you, photographs, and so forth. You might even like to give a little talk." At Laura's alarmed expression, he stopped speaking for a moment. "Only if you want to, of course."

When Laura didn't reply, he carried on. "The other thing I wanted to ask is do you have any other finished paintings?"

Laura thought about the attic bedroom at Auntie Martha's Cottage, with paintings stacked against all four walls.

"Well, I do as a matter of fact," she said.

"Would you consider allowing us to exhibit them here? There is enormous interest in them right now."

"Well, yes, of course," she said, in a small, faraway voice. Shock seemed to have tied her larynx in knots.

"And I have one other great favour to ask you." He leant forward even further, decreasing the distance between them. Laura instinctively leaned back to compensate. "Would you consider loaning us the Buddleia, just for a few months?"

She shook her head, but it wasn't a negative gesture, more a clearing of her mind. "Let me think about it," she said.

~*~

"So, if I lend him the Buddleia I can go home straight away," she said.

Gary was horrified.

"Well, I'm only staying because I have to pack up the pictures on Friday. And now there aren't any pictures to pack up."

Then she caught the expression on Gary's face.

"I was hoping you'd come with me," she said. "See the cottage. Meet Auntie Martha. You've met the rest of my family." She smiled at him. "We could get the train."

"No need," said Gary. "I have a car."

~*~

The bat lay on the floor of the cave. It was too sick to fly up to its sleeping place. Exhausted by its efforts, it just lay there, amongst the dust and the droppings, twitching slightly.
The bat collector gave a pleased grunt and slipped it into his satchel. Then he climbed up, bare foot, his

toes grasping the rope, to see how many more he could collect from the ledges above.

8. Auntie Martha's Cottage

"Turn left here."

Gary eyed the turn-off dubiously. It appeared to be dirt-track.

"It's all right," she said. "Ben keeps the track immaculate. Your car will be perfectly safe."

"Who's Ben?"

She glanced at him. "He's our neighbour."

Gary was silent, imagining a strapping young countryman with dark hair and gypsy eyes, along the lines of Poldark.

They came to a gate. Laura hopped out of the car and opened it, closing it again after Gary had driven through.

"Pig!" she said, as she got back in the car.

"What? What did I do?"

"Not you," she said, indicating the track ahead, where a large pig was ambling slowly across their path.

"You never said you had pigs," said Gary, slightly unnerved by the size of the damned thing.

"Oh, they're not ours. They're Ben's. We let them graze in our wood and he keeps the track clear and gives us pork. We give him eggs and jam, and so forth. It's a barter economy round here."

Gary liked the sound of this less and less.

The pig was now about half-way across, apparently oblivious to the waiting vehicle.

"He drives us into the village once a week to collect Auntie Martha's pension and shop for the stuff we don't grow ourselves."

"Right," Gary muttered between gritted teeth.

"Is something wrong?" asked Laura.

"No, no. Everything's fine," he said, releasing the handbrake and slowly easing the car forward as the pig made its leisurely way into the wood at the other side.

There was another gate to negotiate a few hundred yards further down.

"To keep the pigs out," Laura said.

Well, that was a relief at least, Gary thought, as he drove the car into a farmyard.

"Oh my God!" he said. "That's a cottage?"

They had pulled up in front of an enormous three storey house surrounded by out-buildings.

"Well, it's not as big as Anne Hathaway's," said Laura.

The front door opened and a huge dog came bounding out, just as Laura was getting out of the car. Gary scrambled out of the driver's side, trying to get to her and shield her, but before he could reach her, she had squatted down with her arms open and the vicious-looking brute was all over her. Gary watched, aghast, as it began to lick her face enthusiastically, tail wagging furiously.

"Oh, Bernie, I've missed you SO much," said Laura.

An old woman had appeared in the doorway and was watching this with an amused expression. She suddenly seemed to notice him and smiled as she came forward to greet them.

"I wasn't expecting you till Saturday," she said to Laura.

Gary wondered why she hadn't warned her aunt of their arrival.

Laura stood up, her hand resting on the dog's head. It didn't seem quite so big now. When it came running out of the house it looked about the size of a Great Dane. Now he could see it was a perfectly normal Border Collie, of the type loved by farmers everywhere. Malcolm's family had two – Sally and Judy. As a child he had played with them, and with their pups. He felt hot with embarrassment at his initial reaction and hoped no-one had noticed.

"I've sold all the pictures, Aunt Martha. There was no need to stay. And I'm rich beyond my wildest dreams." She did a little dance on the spot and then ran forward to hug the old lady.

"And this is Gary," she said. "He drove me up here and he wrote this brilliant article in the Guardian, and Mum and Dad came down to see the exhibition, and it's all just been so fabulous. I've got loads and loads to tell you."

Auntie Martha smiled indulgently.

"I'm so pleased to meet you, Gary," she said, "and so is Bernie."

The dog had come to him and was now sitting patiently, paw outstretched, waiting to be introduced.

"I'll make us all a nice cup of tea," said Auntie Martha.

They were sitting at a solid, farmhouse table, large enough to seat at least eight people, in a room large enough to hold a barn dance. An enormous cast iron stove dominated the back wall, with an array of ovens and hobs worthy of a restaurant kitchen. A blackened kettle sat on one of the hobs. On the opposite side of the fire was a rocking chair, still swaying gently from its last occupant – on its seat was some abandoned knitting. Several mis-matched comfy chairs and sofas lined the walls.

"I'll do it," Laura said, jumping up from the table and fetching a teapot down from the shelf. Gary watched anxiously as she took a cloth and picked up the boiling kettle.

Bernie, the dog, had come to sit beside him and looked up at him expectantly. "What do you think, Bernie?" Gary said, bending to stroke the animal's head. "Will I do, do you think?" Bernie put his head on one side, his eyes never leaving Gary's face, appearing to consider the question, then he laid his head on Gary's knee and licked his hand.

"Bernie is an excellent judge of character," said Auntie Martha as she put a plate of scones on the table and went to fetch small plates, knives and a butterdish.

Laura put the teapot in the middle and went to fetch cups, saucers, milk and sugar.

"How do you like your tea?" asked Auntie Martha.

"Black, please, no sugar."

"Mary Poppins," she commented, to Gary's confusion..

"Tea is tea, milk is milk and sugar is sugar," sang Laura.

Gary, whose childhood reading had never extended to Mary Poppins, consisting mainly of comics and textbooks, had no idea how to respond. Laura grinned at him, "Does that mean you're practically perfect in every way?"

"Take no notice of her," said Auntie Martha. "She's teasing you."

Gary gave her an embarrassed smile.

"Here, try one of these. They're fresh from the oven." She passed him a small plate and pushed the butterdish towards him. He picked up a scone and placed it on the plate. It was, indeed, still hot and the butter melted into it as he spread it on. It was utterly delicious.

"This is gorgeous!" he announced, "It's the best scone I've ever tasted in my whole life."

Auntie Martha went pink with pleasure. "They always taste best when they're still warm from the oven," she said.

Gary, thinking of Laura's wonderful Spaghetti Bolognese and Jägerschnitzel, asked, "Did you teach Laura how to cook?"

Auntie Martha smiled. "She is good, isn't she? Yes, I taught her some things, but so did her mother.

The rest she taught herself. She likes food. What about you, do you cook?"

"Beans on toast standard, I'm afraid," he said, reaching for another scone.

"Ah, well," said Auntie Martha, patting his knee. "You've plenty of time to learn. Now, tell me all about this article you wrote. Did you bring a copy of the newspaper?"

Gary and Laura exchanged a guilty look. "Sorry, I never thought," said Laura.

"I've got it on my laptop," he said, and went to fetch it from the car.

"Laptop?" asked Auntie Martha.

"It's a small computer, Auntie Martha," said Laura.

Gary came back in, carrying his laptop case and unpacked it on the other end of the table. There was plenty of room. "Now, where can I plug it in?" he asked, looking round the room.

"Er – I'm afraid we don't have electricity," Laura said.

Gary stared at her. How could anyone live without electricity?

"Well people lived without electricity for hundreds of thousands of years," she said defensively.

"No, I'm – er – just surprised, that's all." He bent down to cover his confusion and fiddled with his laptop. "Not a problem. It'll run on battery for a while."

He had been going to bring up the actual page of the newspaper, and was momentarily surprised when he couldn't get the internet, but quickly realised that no electricity also meant no internet. "Stupid," he muttered to himself, as he brought up his own typed text.

"Well, isn't that amazing!" said Auntie Martha. "I'll just find my glasses."

"They're round your neck, Auntie Martha," said Laura.

"Oh, how stupid of me. I'll forget my own head next," she said, fumbling her spectacles out of the folds of her cardigan.

After she'd read the article from beginning to end, and re-read the last couple of paragraphs, she sat back on her chair and said, "I think I see a connection between this and Laura selling all her pictures. I imagine you stimulated a certain amount of interest?"

"Yes, look at this." He pulled up a photograph of a queue outside the gallery, then one of a crowd of people standing near the Buddleia. There was a space immediately in front with just one man standing there. "They've painted a line to show where to stand to see the 3D effect," he said, pointing to a yellow mark below the man's feet. "and they're only allowing one person to stand there at a time."

"Good Lord," said Auntie Martha. "The gallery will be sorry to let it go."

"Oh, they're not letting it go, Auntie Martha," said Laura. "I've loaned it to them. What I said was, they can keep it until I've painted a copy and then I'll gift them the copy. I didn't want to sell the original."

She gave Gary a shy smile. "It's become rather special to me."

Auntie Martha, seeing the look that passed between them, gave a knowing nod. "Well, I must get on," she said, standing up. "I need to get some wood in."

"Can I do that?" Gary jumped up from the table. He had nearly said 'Auntie Martha' and then stopped himself. Was that too informal? "I – er – I'm not sure what to call you."

"Call me Auntie Martha," she said. "Everybody else does. Come along."

He grinned at her and followed her along a corridor and out of the back door to a wide, cobbled yard with a huge wood pile in the middle. A large leather bucket stood to one side, clearly intended to carry logs. He picked it up and raised his eyebrows questioningly.

"That's right," said Auntie Martha. "If you could just fill it and bring it in to the kitchen."

She turned to go back in the house, then stopped and looked back over her shoulder. "By the way, are you sleeping together?"

Gary stared at her, shocked. What should he say? Laura hadn't given him a clue but he assumed a lady of Auntie Martha's generation would not approve.

"Sorry," she said. "I didn't mean to pry. I just wanted to know whether I needed to make up an extra bed."

Laura had appeared at the door to rescue him. "It's all right, Auntie Martha. I'll see to it," she said.

As the old lady went back into the kitchen she said, *sotto voce*, "Auntie Martha is very broad-minded. Amazing, really, for a woman of ninety-two."

Gary dropped the log he was holding and stared, open-mouthed. "*Ninety-two?*" He had assumed she was maybe in her sixties. She had grey hair and wrinkles but she moved like a young woman. And she didn't have the slight hump that very old people seemed to develop. He was silent a minute, doing the maths. "And she's your auntie?"

"Oh, she's not my real auntie," said Laura. "She was my grandma's best friend. My mother always called her auntie and so I did too. I've known her all my life. She's my godmother."

"Is that why you live here, instead of with your mum and dad?" he said, thinking how worrying it would be for such an old lady, living all alone in such an isolated place.

"Heavens, no. I live here because here is where I can paint. There's no room at home. And it's quiet here. And there are things to paint. And anyway, I love her."

Another thought occurred to him.

"Didn't you worry about leaving her on her own?"

"Of course not, she's got Ben. He comes twice a day."

"Right," muttered Gary.

Laura took him on a tour of the house. It consisted of two big rooms on the ground floor – the kitchen and what Laura described as 'the parlour'. This second room had rather better furniture and a carpet on the floor. It didn't look like anybody ever used it. "Well, the vicar sometimes calls by," said Laura. "Although, come to think of it, he sits in the kitchen with us. It's a waste, really, isn't it? But," she brightened a little, "who knows? maybe the Queen will visit us one day."

A corridor led off the kitchen to the back yard with another, slightly smaller room to the right. "The dairy," she said. "We use it as a larder. It's north-facing, so it's always cool in here."

Upstairs were four bedrooms and a small box-room. "That's where I used to sleep when I was little," said Laura.

The uppermost storey was one long room with dormer windows. An attic, really. It had accumulated much of the usual junk that materialises in such spaces. Dozens of paintings, unframed, were leaning against the walls.

"Wow," said Gary, inspecting them. "How did you decide which ones to put in the exhibition? They're all really good."

"I just chose my favourites and then added a few with different themes, to give it a bit of variety. Do you think the gallery will be interested?"

"Interested? I think they'll bite your hand off for them."

"I hope it doesn't come to that," said Laura.

Gary had a feeling that there was something missing but couldn't quite put his finger on it.

They went outside to inspect the outbuildings and suddenly it became clear.

Electricity was not the only facility the cottage lacked. The house had no toilet or washing facilities. There was no piped water. Here, behind the out-buildings was a rushing spring with a stone basin. All the water had to be fetched by the bucketful. Now he thought of it, there had been several buckets lined up under the sink in the kitchen. And no taps!

"This is the wash-house," said Laura, taking him by the hand and leading him into a large, stone-flagged building with a huge fireplace containing a large copper vessel.

"We do the washing every Monday," said Laura. "We heat the water in the copper and use this." She brandished a stick with what looked like a colander attached. "It's a posset. You just push it up and down on the washing and it gets everything clean. Then we wring it through this mangle." She indicated a large iron contraption with two rollers and a handle. It looked lethal. "Then we take it to the spring to rinse it and hang it out on the line."

"What about when it rains?"

"There's a creel in the kitchen."

Gary shook his head in confusion. He was under the impression that a creel was a sort of boat.

"I'll show you."

The creel was a long rack, consisting of four long parallel poles, suspended from the ceiling by a pulley.

"Good grief," he said. "This is medieval."

"Victorian, actually," said Laura.

But the worst discovery of all was the outside toilet – a small building clapped onto the side of the washhouse, containing a wooden bench with two holes in it. He peered down one of the holes but couldn't see how far down it went.

"It's got a bucket underneath," said Laura. "You pull the chain and the bucket tips over and empties into a soak-away. When I was little Auntie Martha used to cut newspaper into squares and hang them on a string, but now we buy proper toilet rolls." She waved at an enamel bowl between the two holes. "It has to be a hundred percent cellulose, though."

Gary had turned pale.

"Are you OK?"

He wondered whether they actually sat side by side, then decided he didn't even want to go there.

"I know what you're thinking, and we don't," she said.

Well, that was a relief, at least. There was a bolt on the inside of the door. He checked.

By teatime he had recovered his equilibrium. Laura was standing over the stove, stirring a beef stew. Auntie Martha, having refused offers of help, was busy mixing flour and suet for dumplings, and

Gary was sitting on one of the sofas, playing with Bernie.

There was a knock at the back door. A male voice shouted. "Are you there, Martha?" and another Border Collie came bounding into the room, followed by a man who looked even older than Auntie Martha herself. The two collies pranced around, inspecting each other, with much sniffing and wagging of tails.

"Oh, you're back, lass," he said, spotting Laura at the stove. "And who's this, then. Is this your new beau?"

Laura blushed prettily. "This is my friend, Gary," she said. "Gary, this is Ben,"

He was so far removed from Gary's imaginary country lad, that he almost laughed out loud. He struggled to his feet and stretched out his hand. "Pleased to meet you, Sir."

"Well, he's got nice manners," said Ben. He looked on benignly at the two collie dogs, who had now involved Gary in their greeting, running round and in between Gary's legs.

"I see you're getting on well with Bernie," he said, grasping Gary's hand and shaking it with a strength that belied his aged appearance. "Bernie is an excellent judge of character."

9. The Twin Farms

"I love you," he said.

Outside a myriad birds were enthusiastically greeting the dawn. Downstairs Auntie Martha was rattling and clattering as she stirred the fire into life to make the first pot of tea of the day.

Laura was definitely asleep this time. Her eyes were closed and her chest rose and fell steadily. He raised himself on one elbow and gazed at her sleeping face.

It was, superficially, a perfectly ordinary face – two eyes, nose in the middle, mouth underneath in the usual arrangement. He remembered how his first thought when he first saw her was how ordinary she looked. She didn't seem ordinary to him now. She was utterly beautiful.

Her hair was somewhere between blonde and bronze, the ends lighter, bleached by several summers. It was spun honey. Her skin was clear and smooth, lightly tanned – like fresh cream. Was that weird, he wondered? Comparing the woman you loved to food, as if he were considering eating her?

She uttered a small groan and shifted on to her side, turning her back to him. He gazed in wonder at the way her hair curled on to her shoulder.

"I love you too," she murmured.

They took their morning tea into the conservatory on the south side of the house.

"Nobody is usually allowed in here," said Laura. "This is where I work."

They sat on a well-stuffed sofa at one end of the room. Bernie came bounding in and jumped up between them. "Steady on!" said Gary, narrowly saving his cup from dropping to the floor. Bernie looked suitably contrite, his eyes mournful, but his tail, Gary noticed, was wagging surreptitiously.

"He's really taken a liking to you, hasn't he," said Laura, reaching over to stroke Bernie's head. "I'm just a little bit jealous. He's supposed to be *my* dog."

"No, you're not," said Gary. "It's all part of your cunning plan."

Laura assumed an exaggeratedly innocent expression. "I don't know what you're talking about."

"You intend to kidnap me and force me to write articles on how marvellous you are."

She punched him on the shoulder and this time his cup wobbled dangerously on his saucer.

"Actually, that's not a bad idea."

Gary surveyed the studio. The working area took up a tiny fraction of the available space – a table and chair, a trolley with paints, brushes, pencils, crayons, charcoals and chalks – all the paraphernalia of the working artist, including a palette, something he'd never seen in real life before. There was a bottle of white spirit, various tins and rags – all laid out neatly. And there was an easel with a half-finished painting of sparrows pecking at crumbs.

"It all looks so professional," he said. "Can I take photographs?"

"As long as I'm not in them." She laughed.

"Actually, that's not my angle," he said. "I want you shrouded in mystery. I'm not even going to reveal where the cottage is. I'm just going to write about your daily life and how you work."

"We'll see," she said, getting up from the sofa,." But first, breakfast."

Breakfast, it transpired, required that they collected the eggs themselves from the hen house. "We'll come back and feed them later," she said, as she slipped her hand under a large brown hen and pulled out an egg. "Come on," she said. "You start at the other end."

His first chicken glared at him balefully and he pulled his hand back in alarm.

"Go on. She won't bite you," said Laura.

Gary wasn't so sure, but he tentatively stretched out his hand again and fumbled under the chicken. It felt like an unpleasantly intimate act. And aggressive. They were, after all, stealing the hens' children.

"No we're not," said Laura. "None of these eggs have been fertilized."

Well, all right, but the chickens didn't know that, did they?

Later, at the breakfast table, tucking into the best bacon and eggs he'd ever tasted, he found his finer feelings had dissolved in the face of greed.

"What do we do now?" he said, leaning back on his chair, feeling replete. He envisaged a busy day helping out on the farm.

"Oh no, you don't," said Auntie Martha. "You can spend the day exploring together. Take Bernie.

I'll make you up a picnic. And I don't want to see you again till tea-time."

They went through the courtyard, past the out-buildings and the spring and into a narrow plain with fields on both sides of the path.

"Is all this yours?" he asked.

"The fields on the left are ours and all the woods beyond. The fields on the right are Ben's."

She waved to the left. "This field is all vegetables – potatoes, cabbages, carrots, tomatoes and so forth; this one is corn, for the chickens; and that one is wheat. We bake our own bread with our own flour."

"Good Lord," said Gary. "You must be just about self-sufficient."

"Not entirely," she said, as they came to the end of the fields and negotiated a stile. Bernie wriggled underneath and joined them on the other side. "We can't mill our own flour. And we have to buy a lot of stuff we can't grow – paraffin, for instance. And sugar. We tried growing sugar beet one year, but it wasn't very successful. These," she went on, pointing into the woods beyond, "are all fruit trees – apples, plums, peaches and so on. The rest of the wood is oak for the pigs."

When Gary looked blank, she added. "The eat the acorns. It's supposed to produce the very best pork. And it means they just look after themselves. All Ben has to do is check on them every so often to make sure they're healthy and getting enough to eat."

Gary had temporarily forgotten about the pigs. Now he looked around furtively, wondering whether he should drop the picnic basket and shin up a tree if one appeared.

"It's all right," said Laura. "They're not in the least bit aggressive."

Further into the wood they came across an open glade with a stream running through. "This is my favourite place," said Laura, dropping down onto the grass. I come here to read and paint."

Gary put the picnic basket down (gratefully – it had seemed to get more and more heavy the further they went) and sat down beside her.

"It's lovely, isn't it?" she said.

Gary leaned back on his elbows and stared up at the canopy above.

"Yes," he said.

After a while they unpacked the picnic, spread out the blanket that Auntie Martha had thoughtfully provided and used it, first as a tablecloth and later as a bed.

"What if the pigs come?" he said, looking fearfully over his shoulder.

"Live dangerously," said Laura.

Laughing, she held out her arms to him and he forgot about the pigs.

~*~

"You know I'm going to have to go back tomorrow, don't you?" he said.

Laura looked shocked. "But you only just got here. And you said you were going to write your article."

"I can't, can I? No electricity. I can't trust the laptop's battery to last long enough and there's no internet, so I couldn't send it off even if I could write it."

"But we're going into the village tomorrow," she said. "You can write it there and send it off. They've got Wi-Fi in the George and Dragon."

"OK," he said. "We'll see how it goes. But I really will have to go on Friday if we're going to fulfil your promise to the gallery."

"What promise?"

"You said you'd give them more pictures. I should take them all. They might give you a whole exhibition room."

Laura thought about it for a moment. "OK," she said. "I'll come with you."

His heart did a little leap of joy. He had been miserable at the thought of leaving her.

He got up and bent down to grab her hand. "Come on," he said, pulling her to her feet. "Let's pack up the picnic things and get back to the house. We need to get the pictures ready today. Then I can text the gallery and tell them what we've got."

"How are you going to do that without a phone?"

"My phone," Gary said, "is right now charging on my car battery."

"Smug bastard," said Laura.

There were forty-seven pictures which Laura deemed worthy of exhibiting.

"Will it be enough, do you think?" she asked. "Or too many?"

Gary texted the gallery.

"We can start packing them up now," said Laura.

Mr Dickinson said forty-seven was ideal and when could they deliver? Gary told him Friday and he seemed over the moon. "We have never been so busy," he replied. "Have you written the follow-up article?"

"Sending it off tomorrow," Gary texted back. "See you Friday."

He had deliberately avoided text-speak, as he suspected Mr Dickinson wouldn't understand it.

~*~

The following day Ben turned up in an ancient Land Rover. Gary eyed it nervously. Was it roadworthy and was Ben fit to drive? He must be in his seventies at least.

"Don't be daft," said Laura, climbing in the back and patting the seat beside her, "He's fitter than both of us."

Gary got in, clutching his laptop.

As they drove away, Laura leaned out of the window and called to Bernie. "You're in charge, Bernie. Guard the house."

The dog sat up, straight as a sentry on duty. Gary half-expected him to salute.

Cruckford was one of those chocolate box villages – all thatched cottages and Tudor beams. Ben dropped them off outside the George and Dragon (full-on Tudor with beams, and mullioned windows) and Gary followed Laura into the dark, wood-panelled interior.

"Hi, Joe," sang Laura to the man behind the bar, who turned round, smiling broadly.

"Hello, lass. I thought you weren't coming in this week."

"I wasn't, I had this exhibition in London, but they sold all the pictures, so I came home early."

"Well done, lass." Joe reached his hand over the counter to do a high five. "And who's this, then?"

He smiled at Gary, who had been hanging back, trying not to look conspicuous.

"This is my boyfriend, Gary," she said.

Gary felt a great surge of happiness. Not just 'my friend' any more.

"He's a journalist. He needs somewhere to plug his computer in so he can write an article for the Guardian."

"Well, bugger me," said Joe. "You'd best come and sit in the dining room. It only gets used in bad weather."

"See you later," said Laura, waving at him as she headed for the door.

"Where are you going?" He had assumed she'd stay with him.

"Library," she called back.

"Library van comes every Thursday," said Joe, as he led Gary through to a large, airy room, set with neat tables and chairs.

"You can plug your computer in here," he said, indicating a wall plug near the fireplace. "The password for the Wi-Fi is G&DCA12. Here, I'll write it down."

And Gary was left alone to write.

He'd finished the article, proof-read it and sent it off to the Guardian, along with photographs of Laura's studio and some of the pictures from the attic, but Laura had still not made an appearance. He got up from the table, stretched and walked around the room, looking at the pictures on the walls. Prints mostly. Constables, Landseers, a few originals by local artists – two of which he identified easily as Laura's. He was examining one of these, it seemed to him to be an early attempt at 3D – two moths on the bark of a tree. He stood back. Yes that worked. The moths suddenly stood out. It wasn't as perfect as the Buddleia but he would have been prepared to pay a substantial sum for it. If he'd had a substantial sum, which he didn't. He cheered up when he thought of the two articles he'd already been paid for, and the other he'd just sent off.

"Oh, there you are," said Laura. "I thought I'd lost you.

10. Gary's Real Life

Laura had an ambivalent relationship with Gary's Sat Nav. On one hand, it released her from the arduous task of navigating – trying to manipulate enormous maps in the confined space of the car, trying to read them upside-down and sideways, trying to see some relationship with the reality outside the car window. On the other the Sat Nav was insufferably smug. It sounded superior even when giving straight-forward instructions. If you failed to follow them it got downright stroppy.

They had met some (unattended and apparently abandoned) roadworks on the way up and had to divert. "Turn right at the next junction," said the Sat Nav and, when they ignored it, repeated the instruction. Clearly it was trying to get them to turn back and follow the original route. This went on for some time before it eventually gave up and said (petulantly), "Recalculating". Then finally, to her relief, shut up.

Laura imagined it rolling its eyes at their stupidity, maybe even stamping its feet.

She was thrilled to bits when they arrived at the dirt track to the cottage and the Sat Nav couldn't see it. It sat, mute, as, according to the screen, they were launched into a featureless void.

Laura imagined it, stunned into silence by the terror of the void, silently screaming, "Oh my God, we're all going to die!"

Not omniscient after all, then.

The experience hadn't taught it a lesson. It was just as insufferable on the way back. When they met the same roadworks (still, as far as Laura could see, abandoned) the Sat Nav started on its litany of 'Turn right here' again.

"Oh, shut up, Delia," said Gary, and switched it off.

"Delia?" asked Laura, "Like the chef?"

"Like my aunt," said Gary.

That rang a bell.

"She of the Baileys?"

"Correct," said Gary, turning towards her for a split second, with a broad grin. "They have certain character traits in common."

"Thinking they know everything and getting stroppy when you don't agree?" Laura suggested.

Gary just laughed.

Getting through the London traffic was the usual nightmare.

"I bet you'd be glad to be rid of this, wouldn't you?" Laura said.

Gary frowned. He'd been agonising for days over how on earth he and Laura were going to be able to stay together. He *would* be glad to get out of London but couldn't see any way he could do it.

"Love conquers all," said Laura.

~*~

Mr Dickinson was over the moon. "These are marvellous," he said, as they unpacked the forty-seven paintings.

Laura watched anxiously. She hadn't quite believed it.

Gary put his arm around her shoulder. "What did I tell you?" he said.

They drove the car round to the apartment and parked it in Gary's dedicated basement garage.

Laura got her overnight bag out of the boot and pulled out another, rather larger, package.

"What's in there?" asked Gary.

"You'll see," she said.

The bread was stale, so they had lunch in the local bistro. Everything tasted bland after the country food they'd been eating for the last few days.

"How about if we try to get tickets for a show tonight?" Gary said.

"No, I don't think so," said Laura. "I think we need to talk."

Gary looked alarmed.

"Nothing terrifying," she said. "We need to plan."

"It's like this," she said, back in the apartment. "I can't live without you. Hell, I can't *breathe* without you. But I can't live in London."

"Shit," said Gary. "I knew this was coming. I don't know what to say. I have to be in London." He waved his hands in a helpless manner.

"Do you?" She was looking at him earnestly.

"It's where the theatres are, the galleries, the museums. I *have* to be here."

"But do you have to write about culture?"

"What do you suggest?" He gave a wry smile. "A series of 'Life on a Country Farm?"

She leaned forward and took his hand. "I was thinking more of your novel," she said. "You can write that anywhere, can't you?"

Gary ran a hand through his hair.

"I have to earn money. I have a mortgage to pay, and all the expenses of this place." He waved the hand in the air. "It costs a fortune to live in London."

She gripped his hand more tightly. "But if you *didn't* live in London?"

"You mean the cottage?" he said.

She nodded.

"But what about Auntie Martha?" For a moment Laura looked non-plussed. "It's her house, after all. She might not want me moving in."

Laura laughed. "Auntie Martha will be thrilled to bits. She loves you."

"How can you know that?"

"I know. And anyway, even if she did object, we could always rent a cottage in the village. It'd be a lot cheaper than this place."

"But how can I pay my way if I'm not working?"

Laura gave him a long, cool look. "If we do this, we're a team. It doesn't matter who earns the money." She smiled. "And it looks like I'm going to be able to make more than enough for both of us. And anyway, how much would you get for this place?"

He hadn't thought about that. Hadn't considered throwing all caution to the wind and selling up. He did the maths. The apartment should bring in a fair bit. Surely he'd at least get his deposit back? And maybe the equity would have grown a bit in the meantime.

It was what you call a no-brainer.

"I'll do it," he said. "I'll put it on the market straight away."

"What, just like that? No thinking it through? No objections?"

"It's like this," he said. "I can't live without you. I can't *breathe* without you."

They grinned at each other.

"I was just waiting to see whether the gallery really thought they could sell all my pictures," she said. " I don't suppose for one minute I'll be more than a nine day wonder, but it should pull in enough to give us a nice nest egg."

Between them he thought they could manage for a long time, maybe indefinitely if they lived at the cottage, but there was still a major problem.

"Do you think Auntie Martha would object if we made a few improvements?" Laura waited expectantly. "Like installing electricity and plumbing and a proper sewage system?" He went on.

She brightened. "I know she'll be all for it. We looked at it and couldn't afford it. But I reckon we could do it now. Between us."

She jumped up and danced round the room. "Hurrah! It's going to be so fabulous."

Gary picked up his phone.

"No, leave it for now," said Laura. "I've got some stuff to do first. Shopping to get. Where's the nearest charity shop?"

Gary hadn't the faintest idea. He'd never been to a charity shop in his life. It made him feel inadequate somehow. "I don't know," he said.

They set off to explore.

They returned a couple of hours later, carrying an assortment of parcels. The charity shops had been a revelation to Gary. Laura had had to prevent him from buying all sorts of unnecessary things. "Later," she said. "Right now we don't want any extra clutter."

They had bought: a large, unglazed ceramic pot, probably a souvenir from a Greek holiday, back in the days when you had an unlimited baggage allowance; a wooden carving of the head, hands and feet (but no definite torso) of a human figure; a small, exquisite porcelain bowl; a larger, shallow, alabaster bowl; and a selection of fresh flowers.

"Now, let's see," she said, unwrapping their purchases. She set about rearranging some of the furniture, floating the flowers in the alabaster bowl and placing the other items in strategic places. The pot she put on a shelf in the kitchen. Then she began unwrapping the parcel she had brought from the car.

"They're your paintings!" Gary exclaimed. "I thought they were all for the gallery."

"These are for the apartment," she said. "Hold this." She passed him a picture of a kingfisher. "It should go above the sofa. A bit to the right. Perfect. Hold still." She made a small pencil mark on the wall. "You're OK now. I'll just screw this hook in."

"You planned all this before we even set off," he said, in a slightly accusatory manner.

Half an hour later they sat on the sofa surveying the results of Laura's efforts, sipping gin and tonic.

"It's amazing," said Gary. The apartment was transformed from a rather soulless, utilitarian space to one of character and taste.

"And it won't do any harm to mention to the estate agent that we have several Laura Kingsley originals on the walls." He winked. "Not included in the price, of course."

"*Now* you can ring the estate agent," said Laura.

To their amazement, they wanted to send someone round straight away.

"But it's seven o' clock in the evening," Gary said. He looked at Laura and she nodded. "No, that's fine. If he doesn't mind, we're OK with that."

"Gives us more time to sort ourselves out in the morning," said Laura. "I'm SO looking forward to going home."

The estate agent was thrilled with the apartment. He gushed. He described it as 'spacious' (Gary and Laura exchanged an unbelieving look). He loved the décor. He was overwhelmed to discover the pictures were by the famous Laura Kingsley. He was exhausting.

"My God," said Laura, after he had gone, possessed of the spare key. "Make me another gin."

The next day, in the car, on the way back to Cumbria, she said, "Did he really say 'over a million pounds'?"

"He was off his head," said Gary.

The wet market was busy, stallholders shouting their wares, the shoppers examining the meat on display. Many of them could not afford the bigger animals, but there was a brisk trade in bats. The seller of bats could hardly keep up with demand. Where was the bat collector who usually arrived early in the morning? He was late today.

11. Settling in

Gary put his laptop to sleep, stood up and stretched. Outside the day was sunny, but there was a scattering of cloud and a new bite to the air. Autumn was coming and with it the bad weather that would drive customers into the dining room. He wondered whether he ought to rent a room. After all, he would easily be able to afford it once the money came through from the sale of the apartment. Despite what Laura had said, he was loth to use her money until he had to.

It had been surprising easy to fit in to the routine at Auntie Martha's cottage. He had taken over much of the heavy work – fetching water and chopping and carrying wood – and he had arranged with Joe at the George and Dragon to work in the dining room every week day from nine till five.

The Guardian had been happy for him to concentrate on a series on the lives and works of the Old Masters, which could easily be researched on line, as well as reviews of new books, which he downloaded to his kindle, thus allowing him to earn enough to cover his London bills without actually living in London. He had visited the city only once in the month since he moved into the cottage, accompanied by Laura, in order to visit the new exhibition of her works. He had written a further glowing article, which had gone down very well with both the gallery and the Guardian.

"I knew the kidnap plan would pay off," said Laura.

Now he felt as if he'd lived at the cottage forever. It felt like home in a way no other place ever had. The only thing he really missed was being able to wash without fetching and heating buckets of water. Renting a room at the George and Dragon would solve that too.

Meanwhile, it was time for lunch. He made his way to the bar.

The food at the George and Dragon was delightful – ploughman's lunches of thick, crusty bread and sharp, local cheese; thick roast beef sandwiches with raw onion and mustard; huge Yorkshire puddings baked in ceramic pots, filled with Cumberland sausage and gravy, which bore no resemblance to the bland, anaemic toad-in-the-hole they sometimes served at school. He realised that he had never really appreciated food till he met Laura. Now he was obsessed with it.

Today, being Friday, there would be fish and chips – glorious fresh, white fish in light, crispy batter, served with golden chips and mushy peas. Laura had laughed when he waxed lyrical about the George and Dragon fish and chips. "If you want to taste proper fish and chips you have to go to Yorkshire," she said.

There was a tap on his shoulder. He swung round and there, unbelievably, was Malcolm. "What the?" he began, as Malcolm said, "What on earth are *you* doing here?"

"I live here."

"What? Here? In Cruckford? I don't believe it. You lived in London last time I heard."

"I'm sorry. I've been meaning to write for weeks, there's just been so much going on. I've got loads to tell you."

"Me too," said Malcolm giving him an uncharacteristically shy smile. "I've met the love of my life."

He gestured towards a table by the window where an exceedingly good-looking young man waved and smiled at them.

"Punching above your weight, aren't you?" said Gary.

"I have hidden depths," said Malcolm.

"Hidden shallows, more like," said Gary, smiling and grabbing his pint from the bar.

"No lunch?" asked Joe.

"I have some catching up to do with these two," said Gary. "Keep a fish for me. I'll be back in a bit."

The young man stood up and offered his hand. "Johnathan Sharpe," he said. "And you must be the famous Gary Brent. I've heard all about you."

"Don't believe a word of it," said Gary. "He lies."

Looking at the two of them standing together, Gary was struck by what complete opposites (at least, physically) they were. Malcolm – tall and broad, with the muscular physique of the farmer's son, fair hair and fair complexion; Johnathan – small and slender with black curly hair and dark complexion. Yet they seemed so comfortable with each other. "A good fit," Laura would have said.

They caught up with each other's lives over the beer and ordered fish and chips all round.

"That was great," said Jonathan, rubbing his stomach appreciatively.

"Shit hot," said Malcolm.

"You still haven't told me why you're here," said Gary.

"We're house-hunting," said Malcolm. "Or, to be strictly accurate, farm-hunting. We're looking for a nice, self-sufficient small holding."

"Going back to your roots?"

"Not exactly," said Malcolm. "We're preparing for the end of the world."

"What!" He spoke more loudly than he had intended and several people looked round. Embarrassed, he lowered his voice. "Have you joined some weird religious sect, or something?"

Malcolm snorted with laughter, then leaned forward. "Climate change, you plonker. You must have noticed. The Arctic ice melting, the Amazon forests on fire. Floods, hurricanes, tsunamis. It's out of control."

"But surely . . ." Gary faltered. "The end of the world?"

He knew about climate change, of course. It had been in the news quite a bit recently. A Swedish school girl had triggered a worldwide movement to make people aware. But he couldn't help feeling it was exaggerated somehow. It was like a scenario from a dystopian novel. These things didn't happen in real life. He felt it had nothing to do with him.

"Well, I suppose . . . I thought someone would do something."

Malcolm and Jonathan exchanged glances.

"We think that's the least likely scenario," said Jonathan. "We don't believe that world governments are going to get together and work on the problems in time to save us."

Suddenly, with an almost physical shock, Gary believed it completely. Just like that. The world was coming to an end and nobody was going to save it.

"Just a minute, "he said. "I need to rewind a bit. What has this to do with looking for a farm in Cumbria?"

"It doesn't have to be Cumbria," said Malcolm.

Jonathan cut across him. "It's like this," he said. "Four possible scenarios. One. World powers get together and work on global solutions – decarbonising the planet, banning mining and use of fossil fuels, investing all they've got in renewables, re-foresting."

"We don't think that will happen," said Malcolm.

"Exactly. We think that's the least likely. Two. The world just keeps heating up until all life is extinct." He gave Malcolm, who looked as if he were about to interrupt again, a quelling look.

"I was only going to say, 'except maybe cockroaches'."

"Right," said Jonathan. "Three. That maniac in the White House will start a nuclear war and finish us off even more quickly."

"And four?" asked Gary.

"Four – and we think this is the most likely scenario – civilization will break down before any of the other scenarios happen. Millions will die, but the planet will survive. Life will survive, including some humans."

"And you intend to be among them." Gary said. It wasn't a question. He almost felt disappointed in Malcolm, as if it would be nobler to die with the rest than try to survive.

Malcolm nodded.

"Hence the self-sufficient farm in Cumbria?"

"It doesn't have to be in Cumbria but we like the area because it's hilly and wooded and we want to be hidden away."

"We expect," said Jonathan, "that when it all breaks down the people from the towns will begin to starve and they will move out into the countryside scavenging for food. "

"Jesus," said Gary.

"So, you see," said Malcolm. "The perfect place would be a small, self-sufficient farm hidden away amongst hills and, preferably, also woods, which would be difficult to detect."

Gary let out a pent-up breath. "You have just perfectly described Auntie Martha's cottage."

Both faces lit up in delight and they said, in unison, "Is it for sale?"

"No," said Gary. "I live there. But if there is anything locally that fits the bill, Auntie Martha will know." He stood up. "Come on, I'll take you there. I want you to meet the love of *my* life. I'll just pick up my laptop."

~*~

The door opened and Bernie came bounding out and threw himself at Gary, who nearly fell under the impact. In the midst of the petting and fussing and tail-wagging, Laura called out, "You're home early. Is anything wrong? Oh – we have visitors."

She came forward, all smiles, to welcome them.

"This is Jonathan," said Gary, "and my old school friend, Malcolm Abrams."

"Well, what a lovely surprise;" said Laura. "I've heard all about you."

"Don't believe anything he says," said Malcolm. "He lies."

"I know," said Laura. And she kissed both of them on both cheeks. "Welcome to Auntie Martha's cottage."

"What nice boys," Auntie Martha said, after they had left. "Such good manners, especially the dark one."

'The boys', as they came to be known had been hardly able to contain their excitement when they saw the cottage.

They exclaimed with delight over the great cast iron stove – "A masterpiece of engineering," Malcolm said. "They built them to last in those days."

"Look at this," Johnathan cried, practically jumping up and down with excitement. "A fast-running spring, straight off the hillside. Beautiful, clear water. Do you drink it?" he demanded of Auntie Martha.

"I've been drinking it for nigh on eighty years."

Jonathan's jaw dropped. "Auntie Martha," he said. "You don't look a day over sixty."

Malcolm had even been impressed by the insalubrious outside privy. "How does the sewage system work?" he asked.

"I dread to think," said Gary. "Auntie Martha called it a soak-away."

"Oh, I think we could improve on that," Malcolm muttered. "I'll look it up."

"You do understand, don't you," Gary said, "that this place is not for sale."

"Sorry," said Malcolm. "I'm getting carried away. You know, you could make this place completely self-sufficient."

"It's practically self-sufficient now," Gary objected.

"Yes, but *civilised* self-sufficient," he said. "Electricity, piped water, a proper flushing toilet, hot water system."

Gary grabbed his arm. "Say that again."

"Electricity?"

"No, the hot water bit. I can't tell you how fed up I am with carrying and heating water to have a wash. I was seriously considering renting a room at the George and Dragon, just so I could have a shower every day."

"But you wouldn't want to drive to the village every day, surely?"

"I already do," said Gary. "No electricity here. I need to plug in my laptop."

"Gary, my man, " said Malcolm, "I think I can make your happiness complete."

12. Civilisation

There was an email from the estate agent in his in-box. It read:

Dear Mr Brent.

We are pleased to inform you that we have received a firm offer of £1,250,000 for your London apartment. This is a little below the asking price, but if you find it acceptable we can exchange contracts on Thursday, 6th June.

We expect completion to take place the following week, as there is no chain.

Yours sincerely

H L Goodfellow

Gary sat back in his chair, feeling slightly stunned.. He really hadn't taken the estate agent seriously. Good God. What was the asking price, for God's sake, if £1,250,000 was 'a little below? Could they have added an extra nought by mistake? And he wasn't entirely sure what was meant by 'no chain'.
.

He was still staring stupidly at the screen when Joe came in with his morning cup of coffee.

"You all right?" he said.

Gary just pointed at the screen.

"Bloody hell," said Joe. "You're a bleedin' millionaire."

Still not quite believing it, Gary replied to the email, saying he found the offer satisfactory.

He drank his coffee and started to pack away his stuff. He had to go home and tell Laura.

But, before he left, he rang Malcolm.

"Hurrah! We're rich beyond our wildest dreams!"

Laura danced round the kitchen, grabbing Gary and whirling him round. Bernie joined in, jumping up and down and running in circles around them. Auntie Martha watched them with a bemused smile.

"But, what, exactly, does he mean by 'no chain'," he asked, once she'd settled down.

"It just means the buyers aren't selling another property," Laura said. "and you're not buying another one. Sometimes there might be a dozen or so people all having to exchange contracts and move house the same day."

What a nightmare! Gary felt he had enough on his plate just arranging to move his goods and chattels to the cottage.

"I suppose I could hire a van and get the boys to help," he said.

"Don't be daft," said Laura. "We can afford proper removal people. Then they do all the packing and shifting."

"How do you know all this stuff?"

"I've got friends who move house," she said. "Haven't you?"

He thought about it. His friends were mostly from school and university. Apart from Malcolm, they were all from wealthy families, people who never expected to move house in their whole lives. He knew at least three whose parents had bought them apartments near their universities to save them from having to live in student accommodation, but none of them had discussed problems with the purchase. If there had been any, it was their parents who dealt with them.

"What did Malcolm say?" Laura asked.

"About moving the furniture?"

"No, silly. About sorting out the cottage."

"He's coming tomorrow," said Gary.

~*~

The boys turned up first thing the next morning and Bernie rushed out to greet them.

"You know," Malcolm said, burying his face in the dog's fur, "what I miss most about leaving home is having the company of dogs."

Auntie Martha poked her head round the front door.

"Have you two boys had breakfast?" she asked.

They had made an agreement on Friday to put in a minimal support system. Enough electricity to power Gary's laptop, charge the phones and run the lights, a piped water supply and a hot water system.

"We don't need to bother with the grid," Malcolm has said, "I'll put in a small solar system and you can add to it later, if you want."

Now, given the unlimited funds available, he suggested a much more ambitious scheme.

"We can put in enough solar power to run everything, including appliances, like fridges and a washing machine." (Laura gave a happy little sigh.) "And we can put some windmills in as back-up. Generally speaking, on grey days there's a bit of wind. And you could have hydraulic power as well. That spring has some force behind it. It'll cost a fair bit, although not as much as paying to connect to the grid, and you'll be completely independent."

It was Auntie Martha's turn to sigh. She heartily approved of independence.

Malcolm stopped talking in order to pay attention to his bacon and eggs, and Jonathan took over. "And I'm pretty sure your stove will have a back boiler, Auntie Martha. These Victorian ranges usually do. So once the water's piped in, you'll have constant hot water."

It all seemed too good to be true.

"So what I suggest," said Malcolm, "is that today I put the small solar system in one of the out-buildings and Gary can work in there while we sort out the rest. Are you OK with that, Auntie Martha? It'll be several weeks' work, I'm afraid. We'll have to put wiring in the whole house and you'll want inside bathrooms and a proper sewage system. I can get a local firm to do most of the actual work and I'll just oversee. It shouldn't be too bad. The house is so big you can still have some living space while it's going on."

"It will be worth it," said Auntie Martha, her eyes shining. A washing machine and running water. *Hot water*. A proper bathroom and a flushing toilet. She had never expected such luxury in her life.

Ben arrived as they were clearing away the breakfast things.

"I just came to drop off some bacon and sausages," he began. "Oh, hello, lads. Nice to see you again."

"You're going to be seeing rather a lot of us, I'm afraid, sir," said Jonathan. "We're going to be working here for the next few weeks."

Ben broke into a broad smile. "Well, I'd better bring extra tomorrow," he said. He looked back on his way out. "And it's Ben," he said.

Gary and Malcolm inspected the outbuildings. "The roofs are pretty sound on all of them," Malcolm said. "So take your pick. Which one's going to make the best office?"

After some consideration, Gary decided on the old stable block. It consisted of two stories – one large space on the ground floor, containing three stalls, and a mezzanine floor above, which had presumably been used to store feed.

"I could have my desk and sofa down here," he said. "and store the rest of my stuff upstairs."

"And we can put a shower in one of the stalls, and knock the other two together to make a kitchen area," Malcolm said.

"I'm not going to *live* here," said Gary.

"Bet you'd like to have a shower and make yourself a cup of coffee, though, wouldn't you?"

"Oh God," said Gary. "How I long for a shower."

"Right. I'll go and get the stuff from the car."

The 'stuff' turned out to be one large solar panel, a battery, some kind of electronic device ("An inverter," said Malcolm), a quantity of electrical wiring and a tool bag.

"Now all I need is a ladder," he said.

To Gary's utter amazement, the boys did the whole thing in one day.

"That's incredible," Gary said, as he fetched a table and chair from the garden and set up his laptop, only to realise there wasn't an electric lamp in the house. Of course not. How stupid of him.

"Hang on a minute," said Jonathan. "I brought some bulbs. No nice fittings, though. Thought you'd want to choose those yourselves." He fixed the bulb to a wire dangling from the ceiling. "Better than nothing."

"Is that safe?" asked Gary.

"Oh, yeah. It's just not very pretty," said Jonathan.

As the boys were packing up to go, Auntie Martha and Laura came out to see them off.

"You know, you'd be welcome to stay here while you're doing the job, " Auntie Martha said. "It seems a shame to travel all that way every day."

"Well, actually," Jonathan said, with a shy smile, "we were going to book in at the George and Dragon."

"Please don't," said Laura. "We'd love to have you, and there's loads of room."

And so the boys moved in.

~*~

"How is your farm-hunt going?" Auntie Martha asked.

They were sitting in the kitchen, Gary and Laura on one sofa, the boys (with Bernie) on another and Auntie Martha in her rocker.

"Not so good," said Malcolm. "We've registered with several estate agents, but none of them have come up with what we want. Your cottage is so perfect it's spoilt us for the other places on the market. It would have been nice if we could have got one in this area, but there's nothing going."

"What about Les Perkins' place? Is it definitely out of the question?"

Malcolm shook his head. Les Perkin's farm was the property they had come to view a month ago, when they'd first met up with Gary.

"It's a nice little farm, but it's too exposed."

"Couldn't you plant trees, or something?" Laura asked.

"No. We'd need to plant a forest around it and they'd have to be mature. It'd be a Herculean task and way beyond our budget."

"What about a high fence?"

"That'd be a dead give-away. It'd just be advertising that here was somewhere with something worth hiding. Don't worry about it. We've got plenty of time, anyway. I don't think civilization's on the verge of collapse just yet."

"I'm not so sure," Jonathan said, gloomily. "This government's fucking everything up." He shot a guilty look at Auntie Martha. "Sorry, Auntie Martha. But what with hate crimes rising and Brexit round the corner, we're getting more and more vulnerable."

"Hate crimes?" Laura repeated.

"People are discontented. A lot of them are struggling and they're looking for people to blame," Malcolm said. "I'd like to get Jonathan in a safe place before it gets really nasty."

"Jonathan?"

"They're getting tribal. Turning on people who don't belong. They're turning on the foreigners."

"But Jonathan's not a foreigner," she objected. "He was *born* here."

"Yes, but he's black. And right now, that's not a good colour to be."

Auntie Martha frowned. She was particularly fond of Jonathan.

"Look, don't worry about it. We'll find somewhere."

Laura had a horrible premonition that she might never see them again. She looked at Gary pleadingly, but he shook his head. He had no solutions. In a couple of weeks the boys would have finished the work on the house and then they'd be off to do some serious house-hunting.

"Well, we won't worry about it now," said Auntie Martha, getting up from her rocker. Why don't we have a nice cup of tea? Or would you prefer something stronger? I've got some very nice sloe gin."

"Don't touch it," Laura whispered to Jonathan. "It's lethal."

Jonathan grinned at her.

Luckily, there was also beer and gin (Gordons, not sloe) and whisky. Gary had stocked up on a few essentials.

Ben arrived to find a party in full swing, and he and Bessie joined in.

~*~

The next day, feeling slightly reduced, Malcolm left the local firm to get on with the job while he took Laura, Gary and Auntie Martha to a huge wholesale plumbing warehouse, in order to introduce Auntie Martha to the delights of indoor bathrooms. The assistants treated Auntie Martha like a queen, offering her tea and biscuits before taking her on a tour of baths, showers, tiles and fittings that left her in a state of wonderment from which she did not recover for several days.

Everything was going swimmingly, except for the problem of finding a farm for the boys. Maybe Providence would provide. Auntie Martha was a great believer in Providence. She just wished it would get a move on.

13. Halloween

October 31st – Halloween. Winter was settling in now. The air was bitingly cold and a white mist obscured all but the nearest trees. In the village the children would be getting their costumes ready for their annual trick or treat. Well, perhaps not quite yet. It was a school day, after all.

The school time table didn't make any allowances for Halloween, or Bonfire Night for that matter. When Auntie Martha was a child Bonfire Night was on fifth of November, irrespective of the day of the week. And May Day was on the first of May. These days they just shifted the event to the nearest Saturday.

Did that go for Halloween, she wondered? Had anyone let the ghosts know?

She shouted up the stairs to Gary and Laura to tell them breakfast would be ready in ten minutes. "Coming," Laura shouted back, followed by a giggle.

"I don't know," she muttered to herself. "Ever since we put the bathrooms in I've had a devil of a job getting them downstairs."

But she didn't mind really. She loved the bathrooms herself. Malcolm had suggested she had her own private bathroom attached to her bedroom. An *'en suite'* he called it. But she had baulked at that. The idea of having a toilet so near to where she slept was disturbing somehow. She'd never even lived in a house with an indoor toilet before now, although she'd stayed in one when she'd visited Ken and Dora for Laura's christening. Twenty-odd years ago now, and she'd never stayed away overnight since. Didn't feel the lack. She loved her home and she loved her life.

The boys and the builders had done really well. They had taken care to change as little as possible. The kitchen had hardly changed at all. If you looked closely you could see where they'd put the electric wires in the walls, and the sockets, discreetly placed here and there. The only other addition was the old paraffin lamps had been replaced by electric standard lamps. The old sink with the buckets underneath had been replaced with a modern double sink and drainer – with taps – and a cupboard underneath.

The dairy had been transformed into a modern kitchen with a fridge-freezer and a washing machine. Already the drudgery of doing all the washing by hand was becoming a memory.

But now all the work was over she was missing those boys. If only they could get a place nearby her happiness would be complete.

Upstairs Gary whispered to Laura. "What time are they coming?"

"They should get here mid-morning," she whispered back. "We'll have breakfast out of the way by then."

"And you're sure she doesn't know?"

They had been plotting this for weeks, ever since Laura discovered that Auntie Martha's birthday was on Halloween. As soon as the electricity was installed she had charged her phone and rung her mother.

"It's just brilliant," she said. "We went shopping yesterday to buy lamps and light fittings. We went to this fabulous shop, well, more of a warehouse, really. They had everything you could imagine. Lovely furniture. We've got standard lamps and bedside lamps and a couple of really nice bedside tables. They're going to deliver them on Thursday."

And she went on to say how Gary had noticed Auntie Martha standing in front of a grandfather clock. The clock was in a dark, polished wood with a glass panel at the front, displaying a brass pendulum. The clock face had a picture above it, and Gary had moved closer to get a better look.

"It's a moonroller," Auntie Martha said. "We had one when I was a child. The moon moves round, can you see? It shows the quarters of the moon. I used to love that clock."

"It's beautiful," Gary said, just as the clock struck the quarter-hour. It had a deep, mellow sound.

Auntie Martha clapped her hands. "It's exactly the same."

When Gary put in his order, he added the clock to the list.

"You could give it to her on her birthday," Dora said.

Laura realised she had no idea when Auntie Martha's birthday was. Why didn't she know? Auntie

Martha had given her a card and a present every year of her life and she had never reciprocated. She felt ashamed.

"It's hard to forget," said Dora. "It's Halloween."

So when the shop delivered the order, Gary directed the delivery men to put the clock in his study. He had considered hiding it upstairs with the furniture from the flat, but it was obviously very heavy and he feared he'd never get it down again.

Now they giggled together, as they came down to breakfast, delighted with their secret.

At quarter to eleven there was a knock at the front door.

"I'll get it," said Laura, and opened the door to Ken and Dora, who were stamping their feet and blowing their hands in the cold.

"It's a bit fresh out here," said Ken.

Auntie Martha stood, mouth open with surprise, a tea towel dangling from her hand.

"Happy birthday, Auntie Martha," said Dora, giving her a hug.

Ken did the same and offered her a small package in shiny wrapping paper, tied up with a bow.

"I didn't know you were coming," said Auntie Martha. "I've got nothing ready."

"All in hand, Auntie Martha," said Laura. "The guest bedroom is all made up and I've just put the joint in the oven."

Auntie Martha glanced at the stove.

"Not that one. The new one in the dairy. We'll do the roasties and the Yorkshires in this one."

Auntie Martha restrained a sniff. She didn't trust the new electric oven.

"Eh, but it's looking grand in here," said Dora, taking off her coat and coming to the stove to warm her hands. "I love the lamps."

"Wait till you see the new kitchen and the bathrooms," said Gary, as he took the coats through to the hall. "I'll show you round."

He was interrupted by another knock on the door.

"It's the boys!" cried Laura, opening the door with a flourish.

And there they were, Malcolm and Jonathan, wrapped up like Eskimos and carrying several bundles.

Bernie nearly had a nervous breakdown trying to greet all these people at once.

The party was almost complete.

Jonathan and Laura cooked the dinner while the rest got stuck in to the pre-prandial sherry.

"When Laura was about two she kept asking why we never gave *her* a pair of teeth," said Dora. "It was ages before we worked out she meant an aperitif."

Leaving them laughing over their sherry, Malcolm and Gary went into the dairy to check on the status of the dinner.

"About an hour," said Laura. "Everything's on except the Yorkshires. Nothing more to be done until they go in the oven – in about," she consulted her watch, "half an hour."

"Right, lads," said Malcolm. "Time to fetch the clock."

"It's really heavy," said Gary. "Do you think we'll need Ken?"

"I don't think so," said Malcolm. "We'll use the wheelbarrow. One can push and the other two can steady either side."

Gary was dubious, but together the three of them manhandled the clock, still packaged in layers of cardboard and bubble-wrap, onto the barrow and made their triumphal procession across the yard. Ben joined them when they were halfway there and Bessie shot ahead to fraternise with Bernie and the guests.

"Bessie and Bernie get on really well, don't they?" Jonathan remarked.

"I should think so, lad," said Ben. "She's his mother."

All four were laughing as they entered the house.

"What's this?" Auntie Martha cried, with a note of alarm, as they wheeled the barrow into her nice, clean kitchen.

"You'll see," said Laura, as they watched the boys manoeuvre the package into a convenient space between the sofas.

"Oh," she gasped, as they ripped the cardboard away to reveal the clock. "Oh my God!"

And, to everyone's surprise, including her own, she burst into tears.

"Oh, God, I'm really sorry, Auntie Martha. Don't you like it? I can always send it back." Gary was beside himself.

"My darling boy, said Auntie Martha, reaching up to pat his cheek, "Of course I like it. I love it. It just brought back memories, that's all. Thank you so much. It will make me happy every time I look at it."

What had actually happened was that seeing the clock standing there in her own kitchen had prompted a sudden, startlingly clear memory of her father lifting her up to see the moon move round, and showing her where the key went in to wind it up. "I have to wind it once a week," he said. "It's an eight day clock." Which confused the four year old Martha, who already knew there were seven days in a week. It was one of the few moments of intimacy she had shared with her father, who was not an approachable man.

Twelve years later she had left home to go and work as a land girl without having ever made a close relationship with him. Now she regretted not having tried harder.

In November 1945, having survived the war without a scratch, her family home had been blown up, not by a bomb but by an exploding gas main. Nothing had survived the resulting conflagration, including both her parents, who had been sitting in the living room listening to the wireless at the time. They had only paid off the mortgage the week before. And Auntie Martha been left with nothing from her old family home – not even a teaspoon.

"I love it," she repeated. And Gary smiled, happy that he hadn't made a dreadful mistake.

The dinner was excellent, despite the joint being cooked in the dubious electric oven. Even the Yorkshires were very nearly as good as her own. She had offered to take over but been flatly refused. "You're doing no work on your birthday," Laura said. And Jonathan had backed her up. Such a lovely boy!

All through the meal her eyes kept straying to the beautiful clock. What a wonderful thing to do! She had liked Gary on sight and everything she had learned about him since confirmed her opinion. He made a loving and loyal partner for Laura. They would have beautiful children and, God willing, she might even live to see them.

She read only recently of a woman who had died at the age of 120. She had smoked like a chimney all her life and declared she only had one wrinkle and she was sitting on it!

Martha herself had plenty of wrinkles but she still felt young. Maybe that was the secret. She caught Ben's eye across the table. He was smiling at her and she suspected he knew what she was thinking. Ben too. He was sailing through old age still as fit as ever. Maybe inside every old person there was a young person fighting to get out.

They went to bed that night happily tipsy and full of bonhomie.

The only cloud on the horizon was that tomorrow the boys would leave for good.

14. Providence Steps in

The next morning dawned as cold as ever. The trees that could be seen through the mist had frost limning their branches.

Auntie Martha let Bernie out to do his business and then, gratefully, used the downstairs toilet. What a blessing that was. Such a joy not having to brave the cold in her dressing gown. And nice to be far enough away from the bedrooms to be reasonably sure no-one would hear her.

The house was lovely and warm. One of the things Malcolm had installed was insulation. It was amazing what a difference it made. "See how it goes," he had said. "If you're not warm enough this winter, we can always put in a hot air system."

But so far she had not needed to light the paraffin stoves and it didn't get much colder than this.

Bernie came back in, cold and damp from the mist and she rubbed him down with a towel.

"Well, what do you think, Bernie?" she asked, as she poured her first cup of tea. "Is it warm enough?"

Bernie agreed that it was and settled down beside her chair. She stroked his fur absent-mindedly as she waited for the others to come down.

Jonathan was first. "Ah, tea!" he cried, grabbing a cup from the shelf and helping himself. "Have you had breakfast yet?"

"Certainly not," said Auntie Martha. "I'm waiting for the rest to get up."

"I suspect that may be some time," said Jonathan. "Shall I make some toast to be going on with?"

Breakfast turned out to be a long, drawn-out affair as the others drifted in in ones and twos, stretching and yawning.

"It's too comfortable, that's the trouble," said Ken. "I didn't want to get out of bed."

"Well, it's better than not wanting to get out of bed because it's too cold," said Dora.

Auntie Martha nodded. Many's the morning she had woken up to ice on the inside of the windows.

A dog barked outside and she looked up, expecting to hear Ben's knock at the back door. But it didn't come and the dog barked again.

"Bessie," she said, getting up from her chair. But Dora beat her to it. The dog was barking outside, turning in a circle and heading back the way she came, looking back at Dora in a clear invitation to her to follow.

"I'll get my coat," she said.

"I'll get the car," said Malcolm. Ben's farm was a twenty minute walk away. Bessie was already racing ahead and was half-way there when he caught up with her. "Hop in," he said, opening the passenger door, and Bessie jumped up beside him, whining anxiously in the back of her throat. "It's all right, old girl," he said. "We'll be there in two wags of a tail."

The others followed at a more sedate pace – Ken, Dora and Auntie Martha in one car, Gary, Laura and Jonathan in the other.

Ben was lying at the bottom of the stairs, one leg twisted under him. Malcolm knelt beside him and gave a great sigh of relief as he realised the old man was still breathing. "You all right, you old bugger?" he asked.

Ben opened his eyes. "I've been better," he said. "Bloody stair carpet. I've been meaning to fix it for ages. Here, give me a hand up."

"Oh, no you don't," said Malcolm. "You can bloody well stay where you are till the ambulance arrives."

He pulled his phone out of his pocket.

"I'll be all right," Ben protested weakly. "I just need a hand up, that's all."

"You will stay exactly where you are." Auntie Martha's voice echoed through the old house. Defeated, Ben lay back. "Get cushions and blankets!"

Everyone leapt to her bidding and Ben was soon tucked in and made comfortable.

Laura busied herself lighting his stove and putting the kettle on.

Jonathan made a fuss of Bessie. "Brave girl," he said. "Well done."

Malcolm left them to it and headed for the door.

"Where are you going?" Laura asked.

"I'm going to the front gate to meet the ambulance," he said. "They'll never find us otherwise."

"I'll come with you," said Gary, sensing his presence was not required.

The ambulance men were bemused by the crowd of people in attendance.

"What's happened here, then?" one of them said.

"Nothing, lad," said Ben from his cocoon of blankets. "I just fell down the stairs, that's all. It's a lot of fuss about nothing."

"We'll see about that," said the ambulance man, kneeling down and probing Ben with quick, professional movements.

"He's not broken his neck or his back," he said, standing up and brushing dust off his uniform. "We can move him."

His colleague was already coming in to the house, carrying a stretcher.

Still protesting, Ben was loaded into the ambulance.

"Can I come with him?" asked Auntie Martha.

"Of course, love," said the taller of the two. I'll just get him settled."

The ambulance drove off and Laura served tea to the remaining contingent. Malcolm went back to his car and returned with his toolbox.

"What are you doing?" Laura asked.

"Fixing the bloody stair carpet," he said, between clenched teeth.

"We should go and join them at the hospital," Laura said to Gary.

"No, wait a minute," said Malcolm. "What needs doing on the farm? Are there animals to be fed?"

"The chickens," said Laura, ashamed that she hadn't thought of that herself. "And the cow needs milking. I'd better do that before I go."

"I'll do it," said Malcolm. "Just show me where they are."

"You don't know how to milk a cow, do you?"

"I grew up on a dairy farm," said Malcolm. "I've been milking cows since I was old enough to walk."

Malcolm and Jonathan stayed behind to look after Ben's farm, while the others went to the hospital. They found Auntie Martha in a waiting room, fretting because she hadn't thought to bring her knitting.

"He's being X-rayed," she said. "The ambulance man reckons he's broken his leg, and maybe his pelvis but they won't know till they've looked at the X-rays. I don't know. I really don't know how he'll manage. I can't run both farms. What if they won't let him out of hospital?"

Laura and Gary exchanged glances.

"I'll ring the boys," said Gary.

Ben was returned to them an hour and a half later, wrapped in a blanket and installed in a wheel chair, his leg in a plaster cast, stuck out in front of him. He was beside himself with worry about his cow. "She needs milking," he said. "She has to be milked or she'll be in pain. I've got to get back."

"It's OK," said Gary. "The boys are seeing to it. Malcolm's already milked her and Jonathan's fed the chickens. Is there anything else needs doing?"

Ben glared at him. "Malcolm's milked Daisy? Does he know what he's doing?"

"He grew up on a dairy farm. He's been milking cows all his life."

Ben heaved a great sigh of relief. "I don't mind telling you, lad. I love that cow like she was family." He put his head in his hands. "I don't know how I'm going to manage."

"Well, the boys said, if you like, they'll stay with you until you're up and about again. All you have to do is tell them what needs doing and they'll see to it."

Ben shook his head. "I can't afford to pay them," he said. "The farm only pays its way. I haven't anything extra."

"They don't want paying, Ben," said Gary. "They're your friends."

"But what about their jobs? They can't just drop everything and move in with me."

"Yes, they can," said Laura. "They do all their work on the internet. You know, computers. They design computer games."

It was clear that Ben had no idea what she was talking about.

"What it means is," Gary said. "They can do their jobs anywhere. All they have to do is install an internet connection."

"I've told you, I've got no money."

"Relax. They'll pay for it themselves. It doesn't cost much," he lied. "And it means they'll let you go home. What do you think?"

"I think it's too good to be true," said Ben. "But I'm right grateful."

He still didn't really believe it. Wouldn't believe it, in fact, until he spoke to the boys in person. But everyone else seemed to think it was perfectly reasonable, and he was desperate to get out of the hospital, so he agreed to everything.

"Providence moves in mysterious ways," Auntie Martha said, torn between worry for Ben and joy that the boys would be nearby for another few weeks.

"God, it feels good to be back on the job," said Malcolm, hoisting a load of hay into Daisy's manger, and then felt instantly guilty for thinking such a thing when Ben was in the hospital.

"Gary just rang," said Jonathan. "He's OK. It's only his leg, not his pelvis. They said they'd let him out if he had somebody to look after him. I told him we'd do it."

Malcolm beamed at him. "Brilliant," he said.

"Right," said Jonathan, returning the beam. " Do we need to do anything else here?"

"Just stoke up the fire, will you? And bring the water in. I'll finish up here, and then we can go back to the cottage and have a bite to eat. I'm starving."

"I noticed there was a fair bit of meat left on the joint," said Jonathan. "Why don't you stay here and wait for Ben, and I'll bring sandwiches."

Two hours later a convoy of ambulance and two cars came up the track between the farms. Jonathan had laid out a huge quantity of food on Ben's kitchen table.

"Oh, joy!" cried Laura. "All we could get was horrible limp sandwiches from a machine. I'm ravenous."

They settled Ben's wheelchair in front of the table and fed him beef sandwiches.

"Is it right that you'll stay with me?" he asked, pulling Jonathan's sleeve as he went past.

"Of course," said Jonathan. "Glad to. It'll be good practise for us."

"Malcolm and Jonathan want to live on a farm just like this one," Laura said. "They've been looking for ages."

"Have you now?" said Ben.

"Yes we have," said Jonathan. "And we're really glad to practise on yours."

"Well, I'm right grateful, lad." Ben's voice was gruff with emotion.

"Then let's just celebrate Ben's safe return," said Malcolm. "I just happen to have a selection of beverages here. Bar's open."

Laura put the kettle on for those who preferred something a little weaker.

Ben put his hand up as she walked past and she bent down to listen as he whispered, "I've only got one spare bedroom. Do you think they'll mind sharing?"

Laura smiled. "I'm sure they won't mind at all," she whispered back.

~*~

In the wet market, the bat stall stood empty. The seller of bats had not come in today. The other stallholders shook their heads. No doubt he had sold so many bats in the last couple of weeks he could afford to be lazy.

15. Ben

Ben stretched his legs out and lay back in his comfortable chair near the stove. On a small table at his elbow rested a glass of water, a knitting needle, thoughtfully purloined by Jonathan from Auntie Martha's knitting bag ("If you get an itch in your bad leg, you can scratch it with this," he said) and a remote control for his splendid new television. Right now he was watching an ancient 'Dad's Army' repeat and laughing uproariously. Things had changed on Ben's farm.

~*~

Ben's great-grandfather had built the twin farms for his two younger sons. At that time, the family had owned vast tracts of land. The eldest son had inherited the family home, eventually appropriated during the Great War as a forces hospital and now one of the less popular stately homes owned by the National Trust. But the twin farms he built for his two younger sons survived as working smallholdings. The other son had sold his and moved away after his father's death, but Ben's grandfather had stayed and continued to work the farm. It had never been particularly profitable but it had sustained the family through the Depression and the Second World War and was sustaining Ben still.

His father had not volunteered for the second great war and was not conscripted, as farming was a reserved occupation. Just as well, since his young wife had died soon after giving birth to their only son and he had his hands full raising the child and providing food for the war effort.

The pigs had been an inspiration, needing very little care, since they fed themselves by foraging. He had made a deal with the new owner of his uncle's erstwhile farm and the pigs had free range in the woods of both properties. In return he had maintained the tracks of both properties and supplied Mr Hathersage and his wife with much appreciated extra rations of pork. The arrangement had continued after the deaths of both men and into the next generation.

Ben had been very fond of Mrs Hathersage. Being childless herself, she had made much of him. He took to calling in to see her most days on his way home from school. She gave him cake, something he never got at home – his father's cooking was very basic – and he spent many a happy hour playing with her cats. Sometimes in bad weather she would drive him to school in her pony and trap, and pick him up at the end of the day. She mothered the motherless boy and he loved her. It never crossed his mind how very old she was and that she would die one day. So, when he found her lying down on the kitchen floor, he assumed she was asleep.

He was eight years old by this time, but his father had taken him on his knee – something he hadn't done for years.

"She's gone, lad," his father said. "Best say goodbye now."

Ben was familiar with death. Their old dog, Bella, had died the year before and he understood what it meant. It's just he'd never really believed it could happen to people. If it could happen to Mrs Hathersage, it could happen to anyone. It could happen to his father. It could happen to him. And the worst thing was, the thing that troubled his conscience for years afterwards, his first thought was, 'no more cake'.

"Aye, well, you're right there, lad," his father said. "I wouldn't know where to start."

It seemed strange passing the cottage every day (Mrs Hathersage had always referred to the house as her cottage, even though it was just as big as his own house) and knowing there was nobody there anymore.

Ben and his father made sure the chickens were fed every day and collected the eggs. "It'd be a shame to waste them," his father said. And they took Mrs Hathersage's dog, Bruno, back to live with them. He was Bella's son and Brindle's brother, so he was quite happy to come back to his old home. The pony was more of a problem. He flatly refused to leave his stable, so they filled his manger every day and Ben stroked him and whispered encouragement in his ear, but he didn't eat very much, just regarded Ben with sad eyes.

"I think he's going downhill," his father said. "If he don't pick up soon, I'll have to fetch the vet."

Ben knew what that meant. They'd had to fetch the vet for Bella.

"Please pick up, Dandy," he whispered to the pony.

Then, one day, on his return from school, there was someone in the garden – a lady – wearing a big hat and gloves. She was kneeling down and digging with a small trowel.

"What are you doing?" he asked, peering over the fence.

The lady looked up and smiled at him. "I'm planting herbs," she said. "I like to cook."

Ben brightened. "Mrs Hathersage used to make cakes."

"So do I," said the lady, standing up and brushing the soil off her gloves. "My name's Martha," she said. "What's yours?"

And so began a lifelong friendship.

The cats, who had wandered off, looking for better hunting grounds, came back, Dandy picked up and Bruno was returned to the cottage, where he soon ruled the roost. "I never could resist a nice dog," said Martha, as he sat between them, sharing the cake.

The 'Dad's Army' episode came to an end and Ben struggled out of his special chair and hobbled across to Jonathan, who was peeling potatoes at the sink.

"Can I give you a hand with anything?" he asked.

Jonathan grinned at him. "You can chop up the vegetables, if you like," he said, waving Ben to a chair at the table and bringing him a bowl of carrots, a chopping board and a knife.

"I must say," Ben said, "the food has improved since you two moved in."

"I like to cook," said Jonathan, echoing the words of the young Martha, before she was Auntie Martha, when the world was much more like 'Dad's Army' than it was now.

~*~

The day after Ben came home from the hospital, the boys started making improvements to the house.

"Would you mind," Malcolm asked, "if we put in electricity? Just enough so we can charge up our computers and phones and run the lights."

"Oh now, lad," Ben said. "It'd cost a fortune. I'm not made of money."

Malcolm laughed. "It won't cost anything. "We've already got the stuff. We've been building up a stock for when we get our own place. I've got to go back to our house anyway, to pick up our clothes and stuff. I could bring the electrical gear at the same time. And I've got a nice chair you might like to borrow while you're laid up."

It was three weeks later when Ben, searching for the knitting needle, which had dropped down between the seat and the arm, discovered the receipt. The chair had been bought the day after Ben came home from the hospital. He had wondered at the time why a young, fit man like Malcolm, who spent hardly any time sitting still, had bought himself a chair which could be adjusted to lie flat as a bed, or to sit with your feet up. It had come from an orthopaedic supplies shop. He felt tears pricking at his eyes when he realised the boy had bought the chair specially for him, so he could sit comfortably and wouldn't have to struggle up the stairs to his bedroom.

By this time, they had the electricity installed and Malcolm had produced the television ("In case you get bored.") ostensibly also from his own house. Now he wondered if that was true. It might be, actually. The boys did sometimes join him to watch the television.

And then there was the matter of the privy.

"It'd be worth putting one in the house for us," he said. "I know some lads in the village who'd help us put it in. It's just a matter of piping water into the house and putting in a proper sewage tank. Piece of cake."

Ben knew it wouldn't be a piece of cake. He'd seen how long it took to do the bathrooms at Auntie Martha's.

"But that was a whole house," Malcolm said, "with three bathrooms. This is just one toilet."

It was impossible to resist. The idea of not having to go out to the privy in the freezing cold and having to suffer the indignity of being wheeled there by Jonathan, who refused to let him walk outside with his crutches ("Those cobbles are lethal in this weather.") was just too tempting. "Might as well put in a sink and a shower while we're at it," said Malcolm. "We'll get you a plastic stool to sit on."

They did. And a special seat to put on the toilet to make it higher.

Life at the farm was transformed.

And the boys had been so careful with his feelings. That first day (after the embarrassing trip to the privy) Malcolm had wheeled him round to Daisy's shed.

"I can milk her myself," Ben said.

"Yes, of course," said Malcolm, "but I'd really appreciate it if you'd just watch me and check whether I'm doing it right. There's going to be days when you can't do it."

"What days?" Ben wondered.

"Well, you'll have to have check-ups at the hospital every so often."

He needn't have worried. Malcolm knew exactly what he was doing. He thrust his head against Daisy's flank and expertly squeezed the milk into the bucket. The cow moaned with pleasure.

"There's a good girl," Malcolm said as he rhythmically pulled at her teats. "What a sweetheart."

And if Ben felt a stab of jealously, he quickly suppressed it. Nevertheless, he did insist on milking Daisy himself whenever he could. It was something he could do, even with a leg in a cast and he was not one for being idle. And he didn't want Daisy to forget him.

That afternoon Ben was awoken from a snooze by the arrival of Auntie Martha and Laura.

"Just look at him!" said Laura. "Sleeping like a baby. Lord of all he surveys. The world is his oyster."

"He won't be wanting any cake, then," said Auntie Martha.

Ben opened one eye.

"I wasn't asleep. I was just resting my eyes."

The boys were busy elsewhere, Malcolm working on the farm, Jonathan upstairs doing his mysterious computer-work.

"I brought two," said Auntie Martha. "You can share the other with the boys later."

Laura put the kettle on and fetched the teapot.

"I must say," said Auntie Martha, her hands on her hips. "those boys seem to be doing a good job of looking after you."

Ben levered his chair into a sitting position.

"To tell you the truth," he said, "I'll be really sorry when they go home."

"Do you mean that?" Auntie Martha asked, pulling up a chair to sit beside him.

Ben glared at her from under his bushy eyebrows. "Of course I mean it. It's not just the work they do, although, God knows, I'm grateful. It's the companionship. I've never felt the lack before but I will when they're gone."

"You'll still have me," she said, taking his hand.

"Aye, lass. And I appreciate it. It's just – I don't know – having other voices in the house."

Laura, who was busily rinsing out the teapot, wondered when was the last time anyone had called Auntie Martha 'lass'.

"Have you asked them if they want to stay?" Auntie Martha was looking at him with an odd intensity.

"God, no. They wouldn't want to stay with an old man like me. And anyway," he bent forward and lowered his voice to a whisper. "I think they're queer for each other."

Auntie Martha suppressed a laugh. Surely he couldn't only just have noticed?

"Is that a problem?"

"Well, I just think they'd probably rather be on their own, you know. I don't want to be in their way like."

Auntie Martha patted his hand. "It's a big enough house to accommodate more than one group," she said. "I'm in the same boat really, with Laura and Gary. If they want to be on their own they just go in another room. We don't have to tread on each other's toes."

"Oh, Auntie Martha," said Laura, depositing the teapot on the table. "We're always happy to be with you."

"It's all right, my dear. I know that. But I also know you sometimes want your own space." She paused. "And to be honest, so do I. Nothing wrong with that. It just occurred to me that Ben's farm is exactly what the boys are looking for. And that Ben could really do with a bit of extra help." She turned back to Ben. "I think you should ask them."

"I'll think about it," said Ben.

And think about it he did. But he said nothing.

His cast came off on the 16th of December and the whole family celebrated with a party at Auntie Martha's. Ben walked in triumphantly without his cast and without crutches, using only a walking stick.

"Home the conquering hero comes!" cried Auntie Martha, and everyone clapped. Ben blushed as he took his seat at the table.

"He still needs a bit of help for a couple of months. The hospital recommends a lot of short walks, preferably up and down hill."

"Well, that shouldn't be a problem," Auntie Martha remarked drily. "You'd be hard pushed to find a bit of flat ground round here."

"We're going to do it together," said Jonathan. "And with Bessie, of course. I still don't trust the icy cobbles."

"I've been walking on them cobbles all my life," said Ben.

"I know," said Jonathan. "I'm just a mother hen."

After that, all the talk was of the forthcoming election. The boys had high hopes that Labour, under Jeremy Corbyn's leadership, would have a landslide victory.

"Once Corbyn gets in," Jonathan said, "there'll be less pressure to get our own place."

Everyone nodded, except Ben, who looked slightly confused.

"He's going to do all the right things to help stop the world coming to an end," said Laura.

Ben knew the boys were concerned about the climate changing, and it had indeed been a vile winter so far. Terrible flooding all over the country on the low ground. They talked of nothing else in the George and Dragon for weeks. But surely it was a bit over the top to imagine that it was really serious? He indulged them and nodded in agreement when they agonised about the climate. But a lot of it was happening on the other side of the world. Nothing to do with England, surely?

The look he gave Laura was one of silent pleading.

She shook her head. "I don't want to believe it either."

~*~

Meanwhile, in a Chinese city which few people in England had ever heard of, doctors were struggling to contain a new virus, which had sprung from nowhere and was running through the population like wildfire.

16. Election Day

19th December – election day.

Ben woke up with the dawn, once again in his own bedroom upstairs. He loved his special chair by the stove, but he was glad to be back in his own familiar bed.

The sounds of Jonathan making breakfast and the smell of frying bacon issued from the kitchen below. He pulled on his dressing gown, grabbed his stick and began the arduous journey down the stairs.

There was a sense of barely suppressed excitement in the house. Malcolm came in from the yard, pink with the cold, rubbing his hands together to warm them. "I've milked Daisy," he said, "and Auntie Martha will be coming round after breakfast to take you to the polling station. We'll be back in time for tea."

Ben frowned. "Where are you going?"

"We've got to go home to vote," said Jonathan, putting a plate of bacon and eggs on the table. He fetched another plate for himself and began buttering a piece of toast.

"Can't you vote in the village?"

"No, we're registered in Gloucester," said Malcolm, bringing his own plate and sitting next to Ben. "Don't worry. Auntie Martha will take you to the village and you can have your dinner with her. We'll be back by teatime. Maybe a bit sooner."

Ben grunted. He had no idea you had to be registered. He'd never voted in his life before and was only doing it now to please the boys. It seemed a waste of time to him. He carried on eating his breakfast, mildly surprised at how upset he felt at losing the boys even for one day. How was he going to manage when they went home for good?

"I know," said Jonathan. "It's a pain. It would have been much nicer to have all been together. But, you know, the results won't even begin to come in much before midnight and we won't know for sure till tomorrow." His eyes brightened. "Just think, this time tomorrow we might have a Labour government."

Ben gave him a wan smile. In a way, it was something of a relief when Gary turned up to give him a lift to Auntie Martha's. Gary was not quite so intense about this bloody election.

The polling station was in the village hall. A woman swathed in a thick winter coat, scarf and knitted hat was standing at the door holding a clipboard. "Can I see your ID?" she said.

"What?" Ben glared at her. "What do you mean, ID?"

The woman wilted slightly but stood her ground. "You're supposed to have ID," she said. "Something with your photo on. Your driving licence or your passport."

"Doris Crowther, you have known me all your life," Ben growled. "I was working my farm before your mother was born. Since when did you need a photo to identify me? Eh?" He leaned forward, his bushy eyebrows meeting in a frown.

Doris reared back. "It's just Mr Latham said –"

Laura stepped forward. "We don't need ID," she said. "Nobody needs ID. We just need to be on the electoral roll."

Doris stepped back a little further. "But he said I was to ask."

"Well, you've asked. Now get out of the way," said Ben.

"Who is Mr Latham?" Gary whispered to Auntie Martha.

"He's on the council," she said. "Thinks he runs the village." Then, raising her voice and addressing the hapless woman with the clipboard, "Is Mr Latham here?"

"He's inside," she said, "But –"

"Right," said Auntie Martha, marching into the hall and overtaking Ben as he hobbled through the doorway.

"What have you got on your clipboard?" Laura asked sweetly.

The woman held the clipboard protectively against her chest. "I just made a note of the people who had no ID."

Laura grabbed the edge of the clipboard. "Do you mind if I have a look?"

There followed an undignified struggle, as Mrs Crowther held on tenaciously and Laura pulled.

"Come on, Mrs Crowther. Surely you haven't got anything to hide?"

Gary shuffled from one foot to the other, torn between staying to support Laura and a desire to see what was going on in the hall.

"Ah, Mr Latham!" Auntie Martha's voice rang out and, unable to resist any longer, he smiled apologetically at Laura and headed for the doorway.

A large man in a business suit was standing at the far end of the hall glaring at Auntie Martha, who was approaching with the inexorable force of a bulldozer.

"What's all this about ID?"

Mr Latham drew himself up to his full height. "It was a directive from CCHQ."

"May I see it?"

"What?" Mr Latham's eyes bulged alarmingly. "See what?"

"The directive."

Mr Latham glanced right and left, as if looking for support.

"Well, not so much a directive as a suggestion," he muttered.

"And was this suggestion written down?" Auntie Martha gave him her sweetest smile. Gary could see where Laura got it from. Laura herself, still smiling sweetly, was now walking towards them, in triumphant possession of the clipboard, followed by a flustered Mrs Crowther. Ben struggled along in their wake.

"Well, not as such," Mr Latham began.

"And what does that mean? Was it an email? A text message?"

"I – er – I'm not sure."

"So you don't actually have any authority for this blatant act of voter suppression?"

"Steady on!" Mr Latham seemed to be recovering some of his aplomb. "It's common sense to make sure people are who they say they are."

"And is there anybody in the village whom you don't know by sight?"

Mr Latham looked wildly round the room and settled on Gary. "Well, I've never met this bloke before."

"As it happens –" Gary reached into his pocket to retrieve his driving licence but Auntie Martha struck his hand away.

"You don't need to prove who you are, Gary. Your name is on the electoral roll. And, as for you," she turned back to the councillor, who looked as if he was hoping the ground would swallow him. "You can take your watchdog off the door and start behaving with the dignity of your office or I shall report you to the Electoral Commission."

Gary stared, open-mouthed. He had never seen Auntie Martha angry before. And he was astonished that she had even heard of the Electoral Commission.

The other people in the town hall – two people sitting at a desk with the electoral roll spread out before them, and three people standing waiting to have their names checked – had stopped what they were doing and were watching the altercation avidly.

"Look," Mr Latham began again. But he was no match for Auntie Martha and his voice died away under her unrelenting stare.

"Here's the list of people who were turned away," Laura said, passing the clipboard to Auntie Martha.

"They weren't all turned away," Mrs Crowther said. "Most of them took no notice and came in anyway. I ticked the ones who went away. See?"

She pointed to the clipboard. There were a couple of dozen or so ticks on the first page. Laura turned the pages and found a further dozen or so.

"Right," said Auntie Martha, scanning the list. "Just as well we came early. Laura, you can call on the ones in the village and bring them back in. Gary, come with me. You can drive me to the others. And Ben," she turned to her old friend, who had finally reached the front of the hall and collapsed gratefully onto a chair, "you stay here and keep an eye on these charlatans. As for you, Doris Crowther, you should be ashamed of yourself. Get on home and don't come back."

Mrs Crowther scuttled out of the room and, it later transpired, was the only villager who didn't vote that day.

"I'll just copy down the ones who live outside."

"No need," said Gary, taking out his phone. "I'll photograph them."

"I doubt he'll be standing for the next council election," Auntie Martha said, with grim satisfaction, as she buckled herself into the seatbelt. "Now, let's see." She put on her glasses and scanned the lists. "The furthest out is Drakes' Farm, on the Penrith road. We'll start there and work back."

It wasn't as difficult as he supposed. Most of the names were in groups from the same households, so it turned out to only be five stops.

"Well I never," said Mrs Drake, putting a plate of scones in front of them. "I always thought that Mr Latham was a snake in the grass with all his high and mighty airs. Nobody's ever asked us for ID before. Three of my lads have driving licences but none of us have got passports and anyway we never thought to bring anything like that with us. The only one who could vote was our Jack's youngest, who's only just passed his test and carries his driving licence everywhere. I'll just get the butter and then I'll call them all together and we'll go down again. We should be able to vote and get back in time for dinner."

"That's very good of you, Rachel," Auntie Martha said, sipping at a workman's strength cup of tea. "I'm sorry you had a wasted trip."

"Not at all. It was nice to get out and I don't mind doing it again. I wouldn't miss the chance to see that old bugger outsmarted."

The reaction was much the same at the other four farms. One old chap laughed out loud when Auntie Martha described her confrontation with Mr Latham.

"By heck, I'd like to have been a fly on the wall for that," he said. "Still, it's worrying though, isn't it? Do you think they really had instructions from head office?"

"I doubt it," said Auntie Martha. "It's illegal, surely? They wouldn't do that."

"I wouldn't put it past them," said Gary. "And if they've done it here, does that mean they've done it all over the country?"

Auntie Martha looked at him, shocked. "Do you think so?"

Gary gave her a reassuring smile. "Not all the officials are like Mr Latham," he said.

When they got back to the village hall there were considerably more people standing in line. It struck Gary how different this was from voting in the city. When he had voted in London, queues of silent strangers waited their turn. Here everyone knew each other and they were all chatting away nineteen to the dozen. He caught the odd sentence. "'Ah, there you are Mr Latham,' she says, bold as brass. 'What's all this about ID?' And he just caves in and buggers off." "I heard she told him to go home or she'd report him to the police."

Already the story was changing. *Chinese whispers,* he thought. Was that racist? he wondered. Why should Chinese whispers be less reliable than good old British ones?

He took his place in the queue. Ahead of him, Mrs Wellbeloved was explaining to Ben how to fill in the voting card. "You've got the names of the candidates here, see? And you just put a cross opposite the one you want to vote for."

"But I've never heard of any of these people," he complained.

"You vote for the party," she said patiently. "Look, here's the party names – Conservative – you don't want to vote for them, Mr Latham's a Conservative – Labour, LibDem, independent and Green."

"Green?" Ben raised his eyebrows.

"They're all for looking after the planet and going vegetarian and that."

He didn't think they sounded like the right choice for a pig farmer. It was Labour the boys wanted in. And he was only voting to please them. He decided to put his cross next to Sue Hayman.

The George and Dragon was crowded but Joe and his team of extra staff were coping well. Auntie Martha's contingent settled down at a table near the window while Gary went to get the drinks in. He had no sooner got to the bar before the boys turned up. He didn't bother to ask them what they wanted to drink, just added a couple of pints of bitter to the order and made his way back to the table with his laden tray.

Malcolm and Jonathan were laughing uproariously at Laura's description of Auntie Martha's duel with Councillor Latham.

"I can see why the Tories wanted to suppress the vote," said Malcolm. "Workington's voted Labour for a hundred years."

"Apart from one by-election in 1976," Auntie Martha interjected. Gary shot her an admiring glance. Who'd have thought she was so well-informed?

Malcolm smiled at her. "I can see you've been doing your homework, Auntie Martha," he said.

"I like to keep informed," Auntie Martha said primly. "It behoves everyone to know what's going on in the world."

Jonathan was scrolling down on his phone. "Polls reporting biggest turnout in living memory. Great news for us. Labour always does better with a big turnout."

The mood had changed by two o' clock, though. "I can't understand it," Johnathan said. "The polling stations are reporting huge turnouts but the BBC says it was a poor turnout. And there are all these reports on Facebook about people being turned away on one pretext or another. Quite a few say they weren't on the electoral roll. This one, for instance. He says he registered to vote two weeks ago and received an email acknowledging he was registered but when he went to vote they said he wasn't on the electoral roll."

He and Malcolm exchanged a worried look. "Let me see that," said Malcolm, grabbing the phone. He paled as he read the comments.

"They've rigged it," he said. "The buggers have fixed the election. Come on, we need to get back. We've got some heavy work to do on social media, letting people know what is happening and urging everyone to get out there and vote."

He downed his pint in one and stood up. "See you later," he said to the rest, grabbing Jonathan and heading for the door.

Gary desperately wanted to join them, but could hardly leave the others with no transport.

"It's too late," said Auntie Martha. "We just have to hope they haven't managed to succeed."

By teatime, the mood was grim. "How did we miss this?" Malcolm said, almost tearing out his hair in frustration. "Laura Kuenssberg reported yesterday – *yesterday!* that the postal vote was looking bad for Labour."

Auntie Martha looked up. "That's illegal," she said. "You're not supposed to look at or comment on the postal vote until the polls are closed."

All afternoon reports of voter suppression had been flooding the social media but the television news were silent on the issue.

"Well, we've still got to eat," said Auntie Martha. And she set about making sandwiches.

By eight o' clock Ben had had enough and demanded to be taken home where he spent the rest of the evening watching 'Dad's Army' repeats in blissful solitude.

~*~

The next day the house was shrouded in gloom. It had become clear overnight that not only had the Conservatives won the election, including the Workington seat, but they had a landslide victory. While the mainstream media revelled in the improbable result, social media raged with reports of dirty tricks, collusion and downright election rigging.

"That's it, then," Malcolm said. "We're screwed."

Jonathan gave a mighty sigh. "We're going to have to seriously start looking for our hideaway."

Ben looked from one to the other, alarmed.

"It's all right, Ben," Jonathan said. "We won't go till you're completely back to normal."

Malcolm patted Ben on the back and got up to leave the breakfast table.

"I'll go and feed the chickens," he said. "God, I'm going to miss this place."

Ben cleared his throat. "You know, you could stay here, if you like. For good, like. If that's what you want."

Both boys swung round to face him, with identical expressions of hope.

"Do you mean it?" Jonathan said.

Ben looked from one to the other, a slow smile spreading across his face.

"Aye, lad," he said.

And the gloom which had descended on the house vanished as if someone had pressed a switch.

17. Christmas

December 24th – Christmas Eve.

In the grey dawn light Ben was smiling in his sleep. He was dreaming about his father. They were walking in the woods and he was holding his father's hand. His father was naming the trees and flowers as they walked along. His small, child's hand felt safe in his father's big, work-roughened hand.

On waking he felt a sudden, overwhelming sense of loss – as intense as the day the old man died.

He mentally shook himself. Today would be a great day. Ken and Dora were coming for the holiday. All his family would be together. ("You find your family as you go through life," Jonathan said, "and they're not always the people you're related to").

Bessie, who had been sleeping on her cushion at the foot of the bed, sensing he was awake, jumped up beside him and began licking his face. "All right, good lass. I'll see to your breakfast in a minute."

He sat on the side of the bed and pulled on his dressing gown and slippers.

~*~

Ben had always assumed he *would* have a family one day – one he *was* related to. He would have sons who would work with him on the farm, as he had worked alongside his father. He could hardly believe he had grown old and that had never happened.

There had been a girl once – a nice, rosy-cheeked lass who laughed a lot. He'd courted her for eight years and they'd been engaged for five of them, but she'd never quite got round to naming the day. When he pressed her, she just said it didn't feel right yet. She wanted her freedom a bit longer.

And then one day, out of the blue, she said, "We need to talk."

It wasn't what she wanted, she said. She wanted more than the life of a farmer's wife. She wanted excitement, bright lights, adventure.

Ben had just stared at her, unable to believe what she was saying. She had known him all her life. She knew what she was getting. Why did she keep him on a string for eight years?

He didn't understand then and he didn't understand now, fifty years on. It had hurt him and he had been wary of women ever since.

Rosie had left the village and gone to live in London. He'd had a couple of postcards from her, but he didn't answer and she didn't write again.

The engagement ring was in a leather box, gathering dust in the shed. He didn't know what to do with it. He'd thought about giving it to Dora and then, later, to Laura, but it felt like bad luck and he didn't want to pass it on. Maybe he should just have chucked it in the river.

"There's plenty more fish in the sea," Auntie Martha said. But there weren't. Not in his sea. His life was in the village and all the other girls his age had paired off long ago. And somehow nobody else had ever turned up that took his fancy. So the sons hadn't happened.

He had fantasised about the sons he should have had. Strong, capable boys with their father's physique and Rosie's good humour. And he had grieved for the boys that had never existed. Would never exist.

But you find your family as you go through life, right? And he had found his sons at last.

The boys had a long serious talk with him that day – the day after the disastrous election that had caused them so much distress. They laid out their plans before him and asked whether he'd be happy with them. They wanted to hide themselves away from the world that they thought was going to turn nasty. They wanted to make the farm completely self-sufficient. Make it more comfortable, like they had with Auntie Martha's, and build up stocks of the things they couldn't grow or make for themselves. Well, who was going to argue with that? He believed in all those things.

He'd been worried about the cost but they said they could cover all that. They'd been saving for just such an eventuality. They'd look after him and they'd work alongside him and all they asked was to fill up all the outhouses with their emergency supplies. Well, they were just standing empty, weren't they? It wasn't like he wanted them for anything else.

Their enthusiasm was infectious. He wasn't sure they were right about what would happen to the world but he was happy to go along with what was, after all, good housekeeping.

His thoughts were interrupted by a knock on the door and a merry cry of "Rise and shine! Time for your physiotherapy."

"Oh, bloody hell," said Ben. "It's Christmas."

"Not yet, it isn't," said Jonathan. "If you behave yourself I'll let you have Christmas Day off. Come on, I'll do it with you."

He lay down on the floor beside the bed, stuck his left leg in the air, pointing his toes like a ballet dancer, and swung the leg over to the left, then the right.

Ben began to laugh.

"And what's so funny, pray?"

"You put me in mind of Eileen Fowler."

"Who?"

Ben stuck his left leg in the air and pointed his toes. "Eileen Fowler. She believed in keeping fit." He swung his leg to the left. "She was always on the newsreels with her squads of girls doing exercises together – what do you call it? Like the swimming?"

"Synchronised?"

"Aye, that's it. They were a rare sight," He laughed again and swung his leg to the right.

"Ah," said Johnathan, " a latter day Jane Fonda."

"Who?"

"She does exercise videos and urges you to keep doing it till it hurts – 'no pain, no gain'."

"She sounds like a bloody monster."

"Oh yes, she is," said Jonathan, raising his right leg and twirling his foot.

Bessie joined in, jumping on Jonathan's chest.

Ben began to giggle uncontrollably and collapsed back on the bed. Jonathan hooted with laughter, and the pair of them made so much noise that Malcolm came in to see what all the fuss was about.

~*~

The Christmas holidays were coming up, and what with the boys so excited about fixing up the farm and Auntie Martha in a tizz about Christmas dinner and puddings and cake, there was an air of expectancy and jollity that was almost unbearable.

The puddings and cake had been made months ago and were slowly maturing in Auntie Martha's pantry. The cake had to be turned every so often, pricked with a needle and given a libation of brandy.

"I don't know," Auntie Martha said, as she drained the (generous) remains of brandy from the glass. "This cake has taken one heck of a lot of brandy."

Laura and Jonathan exchanged an amused glance, then looked away quickly, afraid they might burst into laughter. But Auntie Martha caught the look and laughed herself.

"Well, alcohol is good for the heart," she said.

As well as the cake and puddings, a huge joint of rib of beef stood marinating in a large roasting tin on the marble shelf in the pantry. Jonathan eyed it warily.

"Will it fit in the oven?" he asked.

Laura laughed at him. "Of course it will," she said. "Victorian stoves were made to accommodate meals for huge households – large families, and servants as well."

"What's in the marinade?"

Laura shrugged. "Nobody knows. It's Auntie Martha's secret recipe. All I know is it's got saltpetre in it. She had a devil of a job replenishing her supply."

Jonathan's eyebrows shot up. "Is it safe? Isn't that what they put in gunpowder?"

"I don't know," Laura said happily. "But nobody's died so far. And I promise that once you've tasted Auntie Martha's Christmas beef you'll be her slave for life."

Jonathan looked at her with a deadly serious expression and said, "I already am."

~*~

After breakfast, Ben and the boys set off, armed with thick leather gloves and pruning shears, to cut some holly. As they went along, Ben named the trees and flowers. He had never been so happy.

They had barely got the decorations in place when Ken and Dora turned up, wrapped up like Eskimos and laden with parcels.

"By heck," Ken said, divesting himself of his packages and rubbing his hands together. "It's sharp out there."

"Lucky, we're in here then, Dad," cried Laura, running across the room and flinging herself into his arms.

"She was always a Daddy's girl," said Dora, waiting patiently for her turn.

Auntie Martha laughed. "Come on, Dora. Let's have an aperitif."

Jonathan stood behind the table, napkin over his arm, dispensing sherry with all the aplomb of a professional sommelier.

"I say," said Dora.

Auntie Martha's Christmas beef was superb.

"Oh my God," said Jonathan. "If I die, I don't care."

"She won't give you the recipe," Laura said.

"Well she ought to at least write it down for posterity."

"Why should I care?" said Auntie Martha. "I'll be dead."

"Enough of that," said Dora, helping herself to more gravy.

Jonathan, remembering the thing he'd failed to ask before, turned to Laura. "How *did* she get the saltpetre?" he whispered.

"Our local celebrity," said Laura. "You must have come across him – John Evans, the writer. Drives around with a pony and trap. Looks like George Clooney. All the women in the village are in love with him."

Johnathan's eyebrow shot up. "Even you?"

"Even me. I'm only human after all."

Then, at Jonathan's shocked expression, she relented. "Only joking. I'm immune. I've already got the love of my life." Jonathan relaxed. "Anyway, he's unattainable." The eyebrow shot up again. Laura laughed. "No, he's not gay. He's happily married and thus immune. I don't think he even notices them."

"But how come," said Jonathan, determined not to be distracted this time, "he has access to saltpetre?"

"His nephew works in a laboratory."

Christmas was wonderful. They wore silly hats, pulled crackers, played party games, sang songs and generally overindulged themselves. Gary had installed a television set in the parlour but nobody could be bothered to watch it, not even the Queen's speech.

"I feel vaguely disloyal," said Dora.

"Well, I don't suppose anyone's checking up," said Jonathan. (He was secretly keeping up with the news on his laptop but there had been nothing of any great note).

On New Year's Eve they pushed the table against the wall and the younger ones danced. When the Moonroller clock struck midnight, they drank to the future, kissed and hugged and sang *Old Lang Syne*. It had been a proper, old-fashioned Christmas.

~*~

In the Chinese city of Wuhan, doctors were struggling to contain the new virus and the Chinese government issued a warning to the world that the epidemic looked likely to become a pandemic. The warning was largely ignored. Certainly, the little group of people at Auntie Martha's cottage was blissfully unaware of what the New Year would bring.

18. New Year

Dora and Ken stayed for New Year's Day (roast pork with all the trimmings) and finally departed the day after, amid many hugs and promises of an early reunion.

"By heck, it were nice to see them," said Ben, wiping the corner of one eye with his handkerchief. I suppose it's back to the grindstone now."

"It is, indeed," said Jonathan. "First physiotherapy appointment at ten o' clock."

"You must be joking. I've got too much to do."

"Malcolm's looking after the farm. Come on, I'll drive you to the hospital."

"Bloody hell," said Ben, wishing for the umpteenth time he'd paid proper attention to the stair carpet. On the other hand, if he hadn't fallen down the stairs the boys would have had no reason to stay. On the whole, he thought it was worth breaking a leg for. He gave Jonathan a weary smile.

"Come on, then, lad. Let's get it over with."

"You'll be fine," said Jonathan. "You've come on like nobody's business. They'll probably only want you to go for a couple of weeks."

As it happened, it was less than that. Jonathan deposited him at the physiotherapy building and went off to the nearest supermarket to do his first batch of shopping. When he returned at twelve Ben met him with a huge smile. "Just till the end of this week," he said.

"Hey!" said Jonathan, giving him a high five. "What did I say? You're a superstar, Ben."

"Thanks to you, lad. Thanks to you. I'd never have kept it up on my own."

The two drove back to the farm in high good humour, only stopping to tell Auntie Martha the good news.

Back at Ben's farm, the lads from the village were already hard at it, fitting bathrooms and converting the parlour into a modern kitchen and utility room. Ben was glad to get out into the fields and get on with some proper work. Jonathan stored his purchases in the old stable and then went to join him.

By the end of January the work on the house was finished. Jonathan had built up an impressive store of tinned and dry goods in the stable, and now he was starting to fill up an old outhouse. He visited a different supermarket every day, careful not to deplete too many stocks, buying only those things they couldn't produce themselves.

Gary and Laura had been doing the same for Auntie Martha's cottage.

"Do you think it'll be enough?" Gary asked, looking at the tightly packed shelves in what had once been the old wash room.

"Good God, I hope so," said Laura. "How much do they think we'll need?

"Well," Gary scratched the back of his neck. "Three people, one dog and – how many cats?"

"Five, at the last count, but I think Muffy may be pregnant." Laura smiled. "But the cats mostly feed themselves. And then there's the chickens – but again, we grow our own corn, so it'd just be emergency supplies in case we get a bad harvest. I don't know. Maybe we should start keeping a record of exactly what we use each week."

And there was other stuff – clothes, her painting materials. And what about medical supplies? If they were really thrown on their own resources they'd have to be able to deal with injuries and sickness, wouldn't they? The list seemed endless.

"It's not going to be enough," she said.

They talked to the boys about it but it turned out they were way ahead of them.

"This is what I've worked out," said Jonathan, bringing up a spreadsheet on his laptop. "I've divided it into food, clothing, medical supplies, fuel, and sundries, like spare batteries and chargers. What I thought was, we should do an inventory of everything we already have and think about whether we need spares, batteries, etc. What about sewing materials, for instance? Presumably, we'd have to mend things. And Auntie Martha's knitting. We'll need to take her on an expedition to get wool and needles and things."

"That reminds me," said Laura. "She says she's missing a number 10 needle. Can you keep an eye out for it?"

"Shit!" said Jonathan and went over to Ben's chair by the stove. "Ah, here it is." He retrieved the needle from Ben's table.

Laura raised an eyebrow.

"To scratch inside his cast. I forgot all about it."

"Auntie Martha won't be very amused. She's been looking for that for days."

"Sorry," said Jonathan. "Tell her I'll buy her two new sets of every size so she'll never go short again."

That night Laura thought about the scenario the boys believed was coming. She realised she hadn't really taken it on board. It was like a game she was going along with to please them and Gary. But what if it was real? How would she feel about them shutting themselves in and living off the fat of the land while people in the cities starved. And what about her parents? And Chloe? And if she invited Chloe, wouldn't she want to bring her mum and Gordon. And her dad? It was endless.

She was suddenly horrified by the idea of choosing who would live and who would die. What about the people in the village? Would they have to defend themselves against marauding hordes? Would they have to be prepared to kill people? Would she? Did Jonathan have weapons on his list?

"It's all right. It probably won't happen," Gary said. "We're just taking precautions, that's all."

But she was not – entirely – convinced.

~*~

On the last day of January the World Health Organisation declared a public health emergency. The epidemic which had started in Wuhan was spreading across the globe.

"What does it mean?" Laura demanded. "Is this it? The beginning of the end of the world?"

"Naw," said Jonathan. "There's a major epidemic every few years – Aids, bird flu, Ebola. They're getting more frequent but I doubt it'll be what finishes us."

And at first it seemed he was right. The government obviously didn't think it was a problem. Nevertheless, the little band on the Twin Farms redoubled its efforts to build up stores.

There were sporadic reports of the virus. On February 5th, the Diamond Princess cruise ship was quarantined off the coast of Japan. On the 15th the first coronavirus death was reported in Europe. But Jonathan still remained reasonably sanguine.

However, a few days later he had changed his mind.

"It's serious," he said. "I don't think it's the end of the world but it's incredibly dangerous for us. It's running out of control in Italy and Spain, so it's just a matter of time before it hits us."

"But the government says it's not as bad as normal flu."

"Not for you and me, maybe, but it's lethal for anyone over sixty-five. We have to protect Auntie Martha and Ben. The government is lying. I propose we do one last supermarket sweep and make sure we haven't forgotten anything. Then we lock down."

"Mum and Dad?" whispered Laura.

"They should be OK. How old are they?"

"Mum's sixty and Dad's sixty-two."

"Let's not take any chances," said Malcolm. "Call them now and offer them a place here until this bloody plague is over."

But Dora and Ken just laughed. "It's just a flash in the pan," said Ken. "It'll all be over in a few weeks. And anyway we're as fit as lops."

"Lops?" queried Gary.

"Fleas," said Laura. "My dad's family's from the North East."

"Does this mean I can't collect my pension?" asked Auntie Martha.

They locked down.

Laura rang Joe at the George and Dragon to let him know they wouldn't be coming to the village on Thursday. "We're isolating," she said.

"Whatever for?" asked Joe, genuinely puzzled.

"It's because of this virus. It's really bad for people over sixty-five, and Auntie Martha's ninety-three. And there's Ben as well. It's really serious for them."

"Right," said Joe and immediately started worrying about all the other old people in the village.

He was right to worry. By the second week in March, the supermarkets were stripped of goods as the nation began panic buying.

Laura was reading the reports on her laptop. "Toilet rolls?" she said, looking up at Gary. "Why toilet rolls? Why not food?"

"Well, I suppose they're buying food as well," he said, getting up and coming to stand beside her, reading the news article on the screen. "But, yeah, it does seem a bit over the top. It doesn't give you diarrhoea, does it?"

"I don't think so." She went into Google and searched 'coronavirus symptoms'. "Doesn't say so here. Just high temperature and dry cough." She paused to think. "Have *we* got plenty of toilet rolls?"

Gary laughed. "Just check out the old cow shed."

Sure enough, one wall was stacked with toilet rolls, floor to ceiling.

"Are they all 100% cellulose?"

"Cross my heart and hope to die," said Gary.

"Well, we'll be prepared if we ever get Ebola," said Laura.

Laura's phone rang and she panicked, trying to track it down. By the time she found it (on the kitchen counter, under an oven-glove) it had stopped ringing.

"Joe," she said, and was about to ring him back when it rang again.

"Hi, Joe. Sorry. I couldn't find the phone."

"Listen, I've been thinking about what you said, about sheltering the old people and I've set up a service to deliver them a food package every day, so they don't have to leave the house. I was just wondering if you wanted to be in on it."

"Of, course. It's a great idea," said Laura, "but I don't really see how much we can do, since we can't get out ourselves."

Joe laughed. "No, I meant, do you want to be included in the deliveries?"

"Oh, I see. Just a minute, I'll just ask Auntie Martha."

She put her hand over the phone and whispered, "Joe's set a up a food delivery service for the old people. He wants to know if we want to be included. What do you think?"

"Give me the phone."

Laura passed her the phone and listened to Auntie Martha's side of the exchange.

"That's a marvellous idea, Joe. How good of you. Yes, it would be wonderful if you could include us. . . Once a week would be enough, I think. We don't need much, just the things we can't grow ourselves." She laughed. "Yes, by all means, toilet rolls. . . That'll be lovely. Wednesday, yes. . . But I don't know how I can pay you. I can't collect my pension at the moment."

Laura was waving at her. "Tell him I'll pay by online banking."

"Good Lord," said Auntie Martha.

"It seems mean," Laura said later, "to take stuff other people might need when we've already stocked up."

Auntie Martha looked up sharply. "Did you want the whole neighbourhood to know?"

"Oh, I see," Laura said miserably.

"We have to consider the boys," said Auntie Martha. "They've gone to a lot of trouble to make the farms a safe haven. When it does get bad later we don't want people to know that we have stores. We don't want to be a target."

On March 23rd Britain locked down and life on the twin farms settled into a routine. Malcolm and Gary did most of the heavy work, with Ben supervising and doing most of the other jobs. Jonathan did the domestic tasks at Ben's farm and spent the rest of his time working on the internet.

At Auntie Martha's cottage life went on as usual.

Laura took up her painting again but she found it hard to ignore what was going on in the outside world. Every day she watched the news, checked the infection rates, worried about her parents and friends out there at the mercy of the plague.

Before they'd had the solar installed she had accessed the net once a week to pick up her emails.

Now she was becoming obsessive, spending nearly as much time on the net as Jonathan, finding news on social networks that was not broadcast by the mass media. She was horrified by the things going on in the world of which she had previously been unaware. Part of her wished she didn't know. Sometimes she just wanted to go to bed, put her head under the covers and pretend none of it was happening. And all the time she kept coming back to the same question. When it finally came, when society broke down and the world as they knew it came to an end, what should she do? Could she really sit here comfortably ignoring the plight of the millions of people who would die?

"I don't know," Gary said. "It's awful, but what else can you do? You can't rescue all those people."

"You have to look after your own," Malcolm said. "You have to protect the people you love at all costs."

"You just need to get on with it," said Ben. "What else can you do?"

"It's like this," said Jonathan. "Millions of people will die and there's nothing we can do about that, but we can save ourselves and maybe a few other people. We should save what we can and that must include ourselves."

Auntie Martha said nothing at all.

~*~

Jonathan was sitting at his computer, frowning as he tapped at the keys.

Laura, who had come to fetch the milk for the cottage, hesitated for a moment in the doorway.

"What are you doing? Are you still designing websites?"

Jonathan looked up.

"The market's quiet at the moment. Let's me get on with the other stuff."

"What other stuff?"

She pulled up a chair and sat beside him.

"I'm compiling information." He waved at the hard drive plugged in to his laptop. "Anything I think will be useful later."

Laura leaned forward and looked at the screen. It appeared to be a page from a medical journal with descriptions of operation procedures, including some rather graphic photographs.

"Ugh!" she said. "You're not seriously suggesting we're going to have to do this sort of thing, are you?"

"I sincerely hope not. But society will need this knowledge. When civilization collapses, we'll be in danger of going back to the dark ages or maybe even the Stone Age, unless we conserve the knowledge. I've put together a dossier of basic first aid techniques and now I'm looking at more specific procedures."

"But it's all there, already, isn't it? In the libraries, on the net? Why bother downloading it?"

"Because the internet may not survive."

"But –" Laura stopped to think for a moment. "It'd still be there, though, wouldn't it? In the cloud? So, when they get the internet going again, they can access it again."

"I'm not sure about that," said Jonathan. "And anyway, what if we lose the knowledge of how to set the internet up?"

Laura just stared at him.

"Don't worry, I downloaded that information first, but it's complicated stuff. I couldn't do it. You'd need a whole team. We might have to educate people from scratch. And then there's all the other things. We need to know not just how to farm for food, but how to make the tractors and the other farm equipment. How to make everything. Solar panels, electrical wiring, metal pipes – all the stuff our civilization depends on to survive. We may not be the ones to need it, but if future generations are to live better than savages, they will need to learn how to do all these things. I'm building up a repository of information to give the new world a head start."

"Jesus," Laura whispered.

"Although some things might be better forgotten – nuclear weapons, for instance."

"Right." Laura took a deep breath. "How can I help?"

19. The News Behind the News

"You don't need to help with this," said Jonathan. "I'm already using our entire broadband capacity."

"I thought we had loads."

"We have, but I don't want to use too much during the day. The people in the village need it now they're in lockdown. If we start doing mega downloads in waking hours, we could bring the system down. So I just identify the stuff I need to download and then set it up for it to start downloading at midnight, when I imagine most people will have gone to bed."

Laura smiled. "We're country folk. Up with the lark and early to bed."

Jonathan showed her his set up – four computers, each with a hard drive attached. The walls of his study were lined with industrial shelving – one wall already half-full of neatly-labelled hard drives.

"My God, this must represent whole libraries of information."

Jonathan smiled proudly.

"But I have got a useful job you can do. You're already going on social media every day, right?" Laura nodded. "Well, keep on doing what you are doing, post things that interest you, the things you think people need to know. Pictures of kittens, if you like. The sort of stuff everyone else does. Meantime keep an eye out for the news behind the news – the stuff the mainstream media isn't telling us. And tag me in on anything suspicious."

"That's likely to be quite a lot, Jonathan. There's loads of stuff about election-rigging, and about the government giving massive contracts to private companies for things like medical equipment."

"Tag me in. Then I get an overall picture and can decide what to follow up."

"OK," Laura said, doubtfully. "I just hope I don't miss anything important, that's all."

Jonathan grinned. "I expect we'll both miss things that are important. The trouble with this kind of thing is you don't know what it is you don't know. But at least there'll be two of us looking."

~*~

It got worse. Just when you thought it couldn't get any worse, it did. Despite the lockdown, the plague didn't go away, and now the news was breaking about how the NHS had discharged patients back to the care homes in order to protect the hospitals. Tens of thousands of old people had died, alone and in pain. GPs had given blanket 'Do Not Resuscitate' orders to care home residents – illegally, without seeking permission from the families. There were reports that doctors had been instructed not to put COVID 19 as the cause of death. It was assumed that the government itself was issuing the orders and that it was all part of the Prime Minister's policy to simply let the plague run through the population as part of his discredited 'Herd Immunity' policy.

"It's like living in some terrible dystopian novel," Laura said. "It's so surreal I can hardly believe it's actually happening. How can something like this happen here, in England?"

"I imagine Englishmen felt the same way when the Black Death struck for the first time," Auntie Martha said dryly. "Only they probably thought the plague was some terrible punishment sent by God."

"The Ancient Greeks thought that plague followed on bad leadership," Jonathan observed.

"Jesus Christ!" said Malcolm and looked like he was ready to weep.

~*~

Then, in May, the government began to ease the lockdown. Immediately, crowds flocked to the coasts and the riverbanks. Laura wondered if the little group living in the Twin Farms were the only people in the country taking the threat seriously.

She panicked and rang her dad.

"We're fine," he said. "I'm making miniatures and Mum's started going to an arts and crafts group. She's learning how to crochet."

"Oh my God! Is that safe?"

"What? Crochet?"

"No. Is it safe for her to go to group meetings?"

Her dad laughed. "You lot are just obsessed with your End of the World stuff. It's perfectly safe. Otherwise the government wouldn't have lifted the lockdown."

She was right. They were the only ones taking it seriously.

She redoubled her efforts to campaign on line, signing petitions, sharing posts on Facebook, waging cyber war.

By the beginning of May the UK had the highest death rate in Europe and one of the highest in the world.

Laura worried about her parents. She worried about Chloe. She worried about the people in the village. Had the holiday cottage people turned up in droves, bringing the infection with them?

"Some of the regulars did turn up, actually," Joe said when she called him. "But we kept our distance and wore masks. I think they got the message. Most of them have gone now. We haven't had any cases so far."

So far so good. She went back to her campaigning.

In her obsession (it *was* an obsession, she realised that) with the daily infection figures and what the government was doing, or rather not doing, she missed the tweets about the mobile phones. It was Gary who noticed.

"These smart phone people seem to be cocking up a lot recently," he remarked. "First the one that exploded and now all these that are melting."

Laura looked up, puzzled. "Melting?"

"Yeah, Facebook's full of it. They must be using an inferior plastic or something. Loads of people saying the cases are melting and the phones are falling apart."

"I didn't think you followed Facebook."

"I don't really. But people contact me from time to time."

"What people?"

"Chaps from college, mostly. I don't bother with it much. All those pictures of food and drinking parties. And bragging about their careers. Boring stuff. But I thought it was funny that they all got so incensed when their phones let them down."

Laura accessed Gary's page. Sure enough, several people were complaining about their phones. There were photos of phones with the cases losing shape. A couple of which had fallen apart completely. Presumably, the photos were taken with phones that were still functional. Or maybe some people still used cameras. She tagged Jonathan, then scrolled down, reading the replies. It *was* odd.

A couple of hours later Jonathan came down to the cottage.

"It's not just phones," he said.

Once you noticed it, you realised it was everywhere. Phones, iPads, laptops, cameras. And not just electronic stuff. Children's toys, pens, plastic containers, false teeth.

"It says here," Laura said, "that there must be an outbreak of moths. People's clothes are disintegrating in the wardrobes. Is this related? I thought it was only happening to plastic."

Malcolm laughed. "Everything's made of plastic these days," he said. "Most clothing is made from polymers. Look it up. Everything's made of lycra or polyester."

Laura gasped. Her one indulgence was clothes – not expensive, designer stuff, but pretty summer dresses in bright colours. Cheap, plentiful and mostly made from polyester.

"The point is," Gary said, "*Why* are these things melting?"

A vague memory stirred at the edge of Laura's mind. Something to do with a virus? No, not a virus. The other thing.

"What's it called – an infection that isn't a virus?"

"A disease?" Gary volunteered.

"No, they're all diseases," Jonathan said. "Maybe you're thinking of bacteria."

"Yes, that's it!" Laura began tapping furiously on her laptop. "Here, look. I thought I'd seen something."

The article on her screen read. '**New super-enzyme eats plastic bottles six times faster**'. "It says scientists have created an enzyme that eats plastic. There was something else as well, more recently, about releasing it into the ocean to clear up all the plastic. And using it on landfill sites."

Malcolm and Jonathan sat in stunned silence. Gary took a moment to realise the implications and then whispered, "Shit."

Laura looked from one stricken face to another. "What?" she said. "What does it mean?"

Malcolm had gone pale. He suddenly looked very tired. "Everything's made of plastic," he said. "Our whole civilization depends on it. Our communications, our energy systems, transport, the very clothes we wear. Without plastics everything will break down within weeks."

"I thought it was a good thing," Laura said bitterly. "I thought it was a good idea to break down all the plastic waste."

"So it would be, if it were controlled," said Malcolm. "But let it escape and it will destroy the world."

"Bacteria are indiscriminate," Jonathan said. "They can't be trained to only eat waste."

"It's a kind of plague we hadn't considered," Malcolm said, looking round the room at the new electric sockets (made of plastic), the new electric wiring (sheathed in plastic). All their hard work rendered useless.

"If it's bacteria, that's organic, isn't it?" Gary said. "A living organism. Can't it be killed with disinfectants? Bleach?"

Malcolm chewed his lip for a moment. "I suppose you could isolate a small area and keep it disinfected. But for how long? How long before something gets through?"

"It's not as bad as that," Gary said. "Things don't disintegrate immediately. You can see that from the photos. If you regularly disinfected them, you'd preserve them."

"And we're pretty safe here," Jonathan said. "We've already been isolating for months, and this stuff is all pretty recent."

Malcolm appeared unconvinced but said nothing.

Auntie Martha came in, took one look at them and said, "What's happened? Why the air of doom and gloom?"

Jonathan went to fetch Ben and they held a council of war.

First, they had to warn the people they cared about. Malcolm and Jonathan would call their respective families, Auntie Martha would call Joe in the village, and Laura would call her parents and Chloe. Gary realised, with something of a shock, that the only person outside this room that he really cared about was Mr Dale. He called him.

Reactions were mixed. Malcolm called his sister Mary, who was more likely to take him seriously than the rest of his family. She was dubious, but he pointed out that disinfecting anything coming in from outside was very little effort, given the consequences if it turned out that he was right. She reluctantly agreed.

Jonathan's parents, who had become more and more distant when they discovered the nature of his friendship with Malcolm, were less easy to convince. "Well, at least I tried," he said.

Joe, at the George and Dragon, was immediately persuaded. He had always thought of Auntie Martha as the wise woman of the village, and he was very impressed by Gary and his friends. "No problem," he said. "We're already in isolation mode. It's just a case of disinfecting anything plastic. We don't get so much coming in from outside anyway. We got through foot and mouth, we can get through this. I'll just have to warn some of the younger ones to be careful."

When Laura rang Ken, he laughed out loud. "Sorry, love," he said. "I think you've overdone it this time. A plastic-eating plague! Ha ha. Good one. Don't worry about us. Your mum won't have plastic in the house." Laura left it for now.

Mr Dale, however, listened carefully. "Malcolm thinks this, as well, did you say?"

"Yes," said Gary. "We can't be sure, because we don't have enough evidence yet, but it's enough to have us worried."

"Send me the links to the articles. I'll do some investigations myself. I may be able to find out something via the academic grapevines. I'll get back to you. Meantime, how are you getting on in your rustic love nest?"

Laura, still feeling bruised by her dad's reaction, rang Chloe.

"I knew it!" she cried. "It was in the local paper yesterday. Some poor woman was in the middle of ironing when the handle broke and she dropped the iron on her foot. Broke a few bones and got badly burnt."

"Was it a plastic handle?"

"It must have been, they all are, aren't they? And Brian said they've been having problems with plastic for a couple of weeks now."

"Who's Brian?"

"My new boyfriend. He's gorgeous!"

"You've got a new boyfriend and you never told me?"

Everything else was eclipsed by this earth-shattering news.

"Sorry. It all happened rather quickly. You know how it is."

Laura settled down to listen to how Chloe had taken her car for its MOT service a few days before. The young mechanic came out from under a nearby car, smiled up at her and she was smitten.

"I know how it is," Laura said.

"He said I was really lucky to have such a reliable little car and to hang on to it because the new ones were useless. You have to have a computerised thing to find out where the fault is and it's impossible for an ordinary person to do their own maintenance these days. Then he said, when he'd finished doing the service, why didn't we take it for a spin to check it out and, since it was lunchtime, we might as well stop for a bite at this nice pub he knows. And it sort of went from there."

"When was this?"

Chloe thought for a moment. "Tuesday."

"Tuesday! That's four days ago."

"Yes," Chloe said, dreamily.

Laura realised she wasn't going to get much more sense out of her and settled down to listen to a eulogy on the delights of the wonderful Brian. She was almost jealous.

20. Lockdown

Meanwhile, despite the spring lockdown, the virus was showing no signs of slowing down. On the contrary, the British infection rate remained one of the highest in the world. The government had spent billions of pounds on a 'Test and Trace' system, which operated through people's mobile phones. But, despite the vast amount of money it cost, the system simply didn't work. Malcolm was convinced the government would soon be forced to lockdown again and that, when they did, it was likely to last for months.

Laura still tried from time to time to persuade her parents to come to them before that happened but Ken brushed off all her arguments.

"They won't come," she told Gary. "They just think I'm obsessed with some weird conspiracy theory."

"Well, short of kidnapping them I don't know what we can do about it, Sweetheart."

He put his arm around her and she laid her head on his shoulder.

"Invite them for my birthday," Auntie Martha said, as she marched through the room, carrying an armful of bedlinen.

Gary and Laura looked at each other. Halloween was two weeks away. So much had happened since the last one that it felt like years ago.

"Dad, listen. I know you don't want to come while we're isolating, but it's Auntie Martha's birthday soon and she'd really like to see you."

"I don't see how we could, love. We'd have to distance. What's the point of coming if we can't even hug each other."

"Well," Laura began. "You could come a few days early and isolate in Gary's studio. It's got a bedroom and a bathroom and a kitchen and everything. We could meet outside for the first few days and then, maybe –"

"I'll stop you there, Love," Ken said. "You have to isolate for two weeks and that'll be no fun at all. And your mum won't leave her garden for that long. We'll just have to wait till this lot is over."

And that was that.

The reports of plastic products failing were becoming more frequent now. Still mostly on social media rather than the mainstream press and television news. But there was a general feeling of underlying worry.

"The trouble is," Jonathan said, "We have no idea how representative this is. We're looking for it. But the man in the street wouldn't have any idea unless it happened to him personally."

"Look at this," said Malcolm. "A whole twitter feed on inter-uterine devices failing. Apparently they just disintegrate and whatever's in them just spills out. What *is* in them?"

Jonathan looked up. "They work by releasing regular small, measured doses of copper."

"Copper? Is that safe? Surely it's toxic."

"You'd think so, but apparently not. It seems we can tolerate some metals. Pacemakers are made of titanium and that's not toxic either."

"How do you know all this stuff?" Gary asked.

"Jonathan has downloaded the entire medical knowledge of the world," said Laura. "He's probably a qualified GP by now."

Jonathan laughed and shook his head.

In November, the UK locked down again. Oddly, it seemed worse at first, even though the twin farms had never really come out of the first lockdown.

"I think," said Laura, "that, as long as we knew the rest of the world was going on as usual, what we were doing felt like a game. We were pretending to be pioneers, but we could come out any time we liked and everything would be OK. Now I feel like we've gone past the tipping point, somehow. I feel like the world we knew is lost to us. We had a chance to save it, but it's gone beyond that. The virus showed us that we could live a different way. People didn't *have* to travel to go to work. Most people didn't need to go to work at all if they didn't want to. It showed us what was really important – food, shelter, warmth and love. But now, with this plastic plague, I don't see how we can keep going. It'll just eat everything up and we won't have communications or power or even clothing. The cities will starve because we won't be able to deliver food to them."

Gary pulled her towards him and held her. "It won't come to that, Love," he said. "The human race is ingenious. We don't have to use motor vehicles to deliver food. We've still got a canal network. We've still got horses. People managed to live civilized lives before plastic."

"Where's the incentive?" Laura said. "Why would people who live in the country and can grow food share it with the people who have nothing? Take away the consumer society and what have we got?"

"I think we're better than that. You'll see. We'll find a way. Anyway, it may never happen."

Two weeks later the internet went down. It came back up after a few days but it remained unreliable, coming on and off at irregular intervals. Jonathan was tearing his hair out because his downloads kept failing.

"You've got the most important stuff," Gary said. "Just get what else you can, when you can and take a rest in between. About time you knocked off for a bit, anyway. And the phones still work."

On Christmas Day, Laura tried to ring her parents but the phone wouldn't connect. Both the phone network and the internet were completely dead.

For the first time they had no way of knowing what was happening outside.

"Don't panic," Malcolm said. "Everybody else will be phoning their families at the same time. Ring them tomorrow."

Three days later Laura finally got a connection. It was weak and intermittent but she managed to ascertain that her mum and dad were still OK and, as Ken put it, 'having a quiet Christmas'. He said the power kept coming and going, but they were managing all right with the coal fire and a gas stove. He also said he was sorry he hadn't believed her before.

"You were right, Darling," he said. "And I was a bloody fool. That plastic thing. It's everywhere now. We're not so badly off. I've been disinfecting the phone and the computer but a lot of other stuff has just fallen apart. People are going out wearing weird outfits made up of anything that's not synthetic. I saw a man dressed entirely in potato sacks the other day."

"You've got to get out," said Laura.

"It's not as easy as that," her father said. " We're in lockdown. Anyone in a car is stopped and turned back. And a lot of the cars don't work anymore. But we'll try." He sighed. "It's going to be a wrench to leave this place. I – " The phone suddenly cut off. Laura tried over and over again to get through but the line was dead.

It remained dead and the internet never came back on.

21. Surprise

The little group on the twin farms was now in complete isolation. Without the internet and the phone network they had no way of knowing what was happening in the outside world. Everybody else seemed to take this philosophically. After all, they had been expecting this for months and were not fazed by it.

There was plenty of work to do, even at this time of year – animals to feed, wood to chop, the day-to-day management of the two farms. Even Jonathan, who had been directing all his efforts towards getting information on the net, now switched his attention to learning what he could from the material he had managed to download before everything shut down.

Only Laura couldn't seem to adjust. She was unable to settle down to any useful work. For so long she had spent nearly all her time trawling the net and now, without it, she couldn't think what to do.

"Paint," said Gary.

"I can't, somehow," she said. "I stand in front of a canvas and I just feel depressed and inadequate. Anyway, what's the point? Sooner or later my pictures will just disintegrate when the plastic thing gets here."

"No, they won't," Gary said, putting his arm round her shoulder. "If the plastic plague reaches us, we'll just disinfect everything. It got out of control because people didn't know what was happening. *We* know, and we're prepared."

Laura nodded. But she didn't start painting again.

Gary worried about her.

Then, one morning, he woke up to find himself alone in the bed. Laura wasn't in the room. She wasn't downstairs. She wasn't in the bathroom. He looked for her in the conservatory and in his own studio but there was no sign of her. Feeling really worried now, he walked to Ben's farm, but she wasn't there either.

"She'll be painting," Jonathan said. "I bet she's in that special glade of hers down by the river."

Gary thought it was unlikely. It was February and the temperature was well below freezing. He couldn't imagine Laura sitting outside in this, even if she were well-wrapped up. It was only bearable if you kept moving.

Nevertheless he went down to the glade. But Laura wasn't there.

He went back to the cottage.

Auntie Martha was cooking on the range, singing to herself. She took one look at Gary and said, "Whatever's the matter? You look like you've had bad news."

"I can't find Laura. I've looked everywhere. I don't know what to do."

Auntie Martha looked puzzled. "I thought she was upstairs," she said. "I'm sure I heard her moving around just now. I'll just take this off the stove and

I'll go and check. But Gary was already half way upstairs, calling Laura's name as he went.

He found her in the baby room – the little bedroom she used to sleep in as a child. She was sitting on the bed and sobbing.

"Darling, what? What is it?"

She turned a tearstained face towards him. "Oh, Gary, I've really screwed up."

He sat beside her on the narrow cot and folded he in his arms. "What is it?" he said. "Tell me."

She turned her face into his chest. "I forgot about it," she said. "It's prescription only and it ran out after six months. It was the one thing I couldn't stock up on. I got some spermicidal jelly but it was so horrible and so bloody unromantic. I kept forgetting to use it. Oh, it's all my fault. I'm so stupid!"

It took a moment for Gary to understand this somewhat garbled explanation. "The pill, you mean?"

"That's what I said, isn't it?"

Gary didn't argue. He was struggling to think of the right response. His first thought was to thank God that she hadn't been using one of those inter-uterine things that Malcolm had talked about. The idea that she might have a lump of copper floating about inside her with no way of removing it, made him turn cold. Then there was a guilty feeling that he shouldn't have just let her take the whole responsibility for contraception. And then an underlying question surfaced. *Why* hadn't they ever discussed children? That was weird, wasn't it? Was it because they both had busy careers and didn't want children? Or because they thought they had all the time in the world? Or just that it went without saying that they didn't want to bring children into a world that looked like it would end before they had a chance to grow up.

"I – " he began, not sure what he meant to say, when the real point of what she had said suddenly dawned on him. "You're pregnant?"

"I think so," she said, looking woebegone. She curled her hands into fists and thumped them on her knees. "Stupid! I've been so stupid. Heaven knows how we'll manage."

Gary was speechless. He was experiencing so many emotions at once that he couldn't sort them out. Panic was uppermost. They'd have to break quarantine for her to see a doctor – always assuming there was still a doctor available. And what about the hospitals? Were they functioning at all? Was the power still working? And the equipment? As far as he could remember, plastic figured largely. But underneath the panic was another feeling, something primitive and powerful – a savage joy.

"Wow!" he whispered. "Oh, God, Laura. A baby. We're going to have a baby."

Laura was still looking up at him, studying his face. "You don't mind?"

"Mind?" He swept her up off the bed and hugged her fiercely. "It's wonderful!"

Auntie Martha, who had followed Gary up the stairs and dithered at the door, smiled to herself and tiptoed back downstairs.

"I think we'll manage all right," Auntie Martha said. "Gary's right. I can't imagine there'll be much in the way of medical help available, but that doesn't mean we can't deal with it ourselves. After all, people were having babies for untold thousands of years before the invention of modern obstetrics. And you're young and healthy. Anyway, Jonathan's probably got all the specialist knowledge we might need. Are you going to tell the others? Or do you want to keep it a secret for now?"

Gary and Laura exchanged glances.

"They'll know soon enough," Laura said. "Might as well tell them straight away."

"Good," said Auntie Martha, retrieving her knitting, which was something white and lacy and suspiciously well-advanced, considering she'd only found out about the baby a couple of hours before.

~*~

The long winter wore on. Laura cheered up a bit, but she still had a white and strained expression when she thought herself unobserved. She wanted her mother. She'd wanted her mother all along, of course, but now she was pregnant she really needed her. Her mother wasn't a trained nurse, but she'd worked for years as an auxiliary at the hospital and she'd acted as birth partner several times.

If only she'd been able to persuade her mum and dad to come. She kept going over in her mind the things she should have said to change their minds.

~*~

Auntie Martha tapped Gary on the shoulder. He looked up in surprise. Auntie Martha very rarely disturbed him when he was working in his studio.

"What is it?"

"Come and see." She was smiling.

He got up obediently and followed her out into the yard, pulling on his overcoat as he went. March had come in like a lion but showed no signs of going out like a lamb. The day was bright and sunny, but there was a chill wind. This winter had been even colder than the last one.

Auntie Martha put a finger to her lips, took him by the hand and led him to the corner of the house. They peeped round. There, in her conservatory, Laura was painting, and singing as she worked. They exchanged a delighted smile and headed round the back of the house.

"I've got the kettle on," Auntie Martha said.

"Auntie Martha, you've always got the kettle on. Here, let me help you."

"Certainly not. You sit down. I've got some nice Eccles cakes I'd like you to try."

She made the tea, put the teapot on the table, then brought plates, cups, butter, milk and sugar.

"Nothing like a nice Eccles cake straight from the oven to warm you up on a cold day," she said, putting on her oven gloves and fetching them out from the oven.

"Shall I be mother?" asked Gary.

"Don't be cheeky," said Auntie Martha, batting him lightly with her gloved hand.

Gary was just reaching for the first one, when he heard the unmistakable sound of a vehicle pulling up outside. Both he and Auntie Martha froze and stared at the front door.

Then Gary leapt from his chair and ran to the door. "Keep back!" he shouted as he flung the door open. "We're isolating!" Bernie shot past him as a muffled figure, in the act of emerging from the car, stopped dead. The figure bent down to greet the dog, who was wagging his tail and making small, excited whining noises as he struggled to lick the visitor's face.

Out of the corner of his eye Gary was aware of Laura coming round from the conservatory, and he waved her back, whilst he watched the figure pull down the scarf, revealing its face. "Chloe!" he exclaimed. To his left, Laura broke into a run. "No, keep back!" he shouted.

"It's all right," said Chloe. "We haven't got the virus."

Another figure emerged from the other side of the car and simultaneously Gary became aware of Auntie Martha attempting to push past him.

"Just everyone keep still a minute," he shouted, and then, to Chloe, "How do you know you haven't got it?"

"Because we've both already had it. And besides, we haven't seen any other human beings for three weeks."

The other figure pulled down his own scarf and waved.

Ignoring him, Gary shouted. "It's not just COVID 19, what you don't know is –"

Chloe finished his sentence for him – "about the plastic plague. We *do* know. Laura told me ages ago – before Christmas. And Brian knew anyway, because he's a car mechanic and the plastics had already started breaking down then. We have *no* plastic with us. Not in our luggage, not what we're wearing – not even the car itself. We are completely safe."

Auntie Martha finally succeeded in pushing her way into the doorway and came to stand beside Gary.

"Get back," he said, putting his arm out to bar her way.

"Oh for goodness' sake!" said Auntie Martha. "Credit me with some sense. "Hello Chloe. This is a lovely surprise. And is this your new young man?"

At that moment, Malcolm came running round the corner, out of breath. "My God, what's that?" he cried, staring at the car.

Everyone began talking at once.

For the first time, Gary paid attention to the car. It was certainly an extraordinary vehicle. The chassis was more like that of a cart than a car, with large, narrow, wooden wheels. It reminded him of old black and white newsreels.

Malcolm was in urgent consultation with the new arrival. "It's a 1908 Model T," Brian said. "Before plastic was used in cars." He opened the bonnet. "Look, all the leads are sheathed in cloth and rubber. Brilliant, isn't it? You start it with a crank handle."

"Wherever did you get hold of it?" Gary asked Chloe.

"We stole it," she said, proudly.

"Come on, everyone," Auntie Martha said, "In the house. Look at these two. They're blue with cold."

22. Chloe and Brian

Chloe sat in front of the stove, clutching a mug of hot cocoa. She was still shivering slightly.

"It was bloody freezing in that car," she said to Laura. "No heating and the windows leak."

Opposite her, Brian was in animated discussion with Malcolm and seemed not to have noticed his cocoa at all.

"Back in a few minutes," Gary said, getting up from the table and heading for the back door.

Laura looked up. "Where are you going?"

Gary bent to kiss her on the forehead. "I'm just going to fetch Ben and Jonathan. We should all be here when these two tell us what's been happening. They won't want to tell the whole thing twice."

She kissed him on the cheek and waved him off.

At the sound of the car driving away, Brian looked up in surprise. "You've got a working car?"

"All our cars work," said Malcolm. "We isolated long before the plastic plague hit. We've got a working tractor as well."

"That's great," said Brian. "It won't be such hard work as I was expecting."

"Oh, there's plenty to do," said Malcolm. "Don't think you won't earn your keep. We're going to have to expand and put more under the plough this year."

The conversation switched to farming and the group's plans for the future.

Twenty minutes later, the return of Gary with Ben and Jonathan was heralded by Bessie bounding into the kitchen and greeting everyone with indiscriminate enthusiasm.

"Oh, Bessie," said Chloe, relinquishing her cocoa and burying her head in the dog's fur. "I've missed you so much."

"There's another reason for coming," said Brian. "We have dogs." And he bent down to stroke Bernie, who settled his head on Brian's knee and looked up at him adoringly.

"Well, this is a treat, and no mistake," said Ben, giving Chloe a hug and kissing her on the cheek. Then he held out a hand to Brian. "I see you're getting on well with Bernie," he said. "Bernie is a great judge of character."

"Don't be too flattered," said Gary. "Bernie loves everyone. Basically he's just a tart."

Brian laughed.

Auntie Martha and Laura weaved in and out of the assembled company, setting the table for tea and cakes.

"You two sit this end, nearest the fire, " said Auntie Martha, "and you can tell us everything that's happened."

"God, it's so nice to eat real food," Chloe said, grabbing a crusty roll and spreading it with butter. "We've been living out of tins for ages."

~*~

When Laura telephoned her, Chloe was already aware that something weird was happening with plastics. Brian had told her they'd been having trouble with the electrics failing in some cars. The newspaper report about the woman who had dropped the iron on her foot had only served to confirm her suspicions. And now Laura, seriously worried and telling her about all the other incidents crystallised her vague fears into something more concrete.

"I think your friend is right," Brian said. "We should think about this and see what we can do about it. She reckons disinfecting actually works?"

"She's pretty sure it does. And it can't do any harm can it?"

"And she reckons it means the end of civilization as we know it?"

He wasn't smiling as he said it. Perhaps he was quicker to understand the implications. After all, he worked in an environment where the failure of plastic had immediate and disastrous consequences.

"Oh shit," he said.

Chloe was already spending more time at Brian's place than at home with her mum and Gordon. Now she moved to his place permanently and the two set about preparing it as if for a siege, laying in stocks of food and fuel. Chloe decided to spend her entire savings and max out her credit card, if necessary, to make sure they were prepared. "We bought enough food for a year," she said. "Tinned stuff, not frozen. Brian said we couldn't rely on the power. And so I bought a camping stove and got new clothes for us in natural fibres." She opened her (sheepskin) coat to reveal a cashmere sweater. "I got some for Mum and Gordon too, but they didn't really take it seriously. Not then, at any rate."

They had disinfected their electronic equipment and cars on a regular basis, and would have, Chloe was sure, lasted out for some considerable time with careful management, had it not happened that her mum had caught the virus.

"You remember that new strain?" Brian said. "The one that was more transmissible?"

The little group exchanged blank looks.

"It must have been when the internet was on the blink," Malcolm said. "We must have missed it."

Brian shrugged. "Well, the government played it down at first. Then they suddenly cancelled Christmas. Well, they changed it from five days to one day only. And then France closed the border, so obviously *they* were seriously worried about it. The thing is this new strain wasn't just more transmissible it was more severe as well. The government denied it, but they were lying. They knew it was a whole new ball game. They said it was basically the same and that it would quickly be dealt with when they rolled out the new 'world-beating' British vaccine. What they didn't tell us – maybe they didn't know, but they must have had some idea – was that this new strain was immune to the new vaccines they had spent millions to develop. We were just beginning to realise how bad it was when the whole lot came down – no internet, no phones, no power. But by then it was too late for Vera."

"Gordon blamed himself," Chloe said. "He'd gone to a conference. They'd been careful and wore masks and distanced and everything, but there were a lot of people in the building and some of them took off their masks to speak and they all had to take them off to eat, obviously. Anyway, the upshot was, he got ill the week after and was really quite poorly and then my mum got ill a few days after that and she was *really* poorly. By this time, the health services were breaking down. The hospital couldn't take any more patients. And even if they could, what use would it have been? The power was off, and all the other stuff was beginning to fall apart – the machinery, even the bedding and the staff's uniforms. They just said to keep giving them fluids and keep moving them."

Chloe gave a little sob and Brian put his arm round her shoulder.

"We moved in with them," he said. "It was the only way we could deal with the amount of care they needed. Gordon began to get better, but Vera – well, she just got worse and worse – fighting for breath. It was grim."

Then they had got it too. Not as badly as the older ones, but badly enough to make it difficult to keep up the regime of care.

"It was like being in a battlefield," Chloe said. "Day after day just struggling to keep them alive. And then –" she broke off. Laura exchanged a worried glance with Gary.

Vera had died. She had fought like hell. Chloe had watched helplessly as her mother struggled for every breath, her chest hitching and straining with the effort, wild-eyed with the pain and the fear. When she finally subsided, with one last, faint sigh, it was a relief. Chloe kissed her on the forehead and then stood back and allowed Gordon, wild with grief, to take possession of her.

She was grieving too, but mostly she felt an overwhelming anger. Anger with the government for allowing the virus to get out of control, for letting this plastic thing happen. They must have had known something about it, surely? They should have been putting out messages telling people to disinfect. Warning the hospital staff who, God knows, must have had enough on their plate to be forgiven for not noticing this new threat. And also, although she knew it was unreasonable, she was angry with Gordon for being stupid enough to go to a conference in the middle of an epidemic. Her mother had finally entered into a stage of her life where she was happy and fulfilled and now she had been snatched away by other people's incompetence.

Gordon had told them to go back to their own place and leave him to deal with her.

"I'll see to her properly. I'll do right by her. You can trust me," he said. "But you need to go. Get out of here while you still can."

He was in such a state of despair that they were reluctant to go, but he was adamant. "Get out," he said. "I'll deal with it."

"We went back a few days later but the door was locked and nobody answered. We think –" Chloe shrugged.

In their absence, the cars had both succumbed to the plastic blight. Brian had fixed them with new wiring, but that, too began to fail.

"I can't understand it," he said. "I disinfected the wiring before I fitted it, but it was as if it was already infected and it had got right inside."

So they had hung on for a while, living on their stores. Now the power supply had finally failed for good, it was obvious that, if they were to survive in the long term, they were going to have to move to the country where they could grow food.

But it seemed unlikely that people in the countryside would welcome refugees.

"We thought of you, of course," said Chloe, "but it didn't seem fair to burden you." She reached out and grabbed Brian's hand. "But in the end it was a matter of survival, really. We just hoped you'd take us in. The only thing was, how were we going to get to you without transport? We'd have to walk all the way, and carry enough food for the journey and just trust to luck that we'd find safe places to sleep on the way."

"And then," said Brian, "I remembered Sir Piers Bentley-More."

Malcolm frowned. "Why does that name ring a bell?"

Brian grinned. "He's our local squire. One of those families that goes back to William the Conqueror. Lives in a massive house near Haywards Heath. He had the dubious honour of being one of the first people in England to die of COVID 19. He'd just come back from a trip to China."

Everyone looked at him blankly.

"The thing is, he was a friend of mine – well, sort of. He collected vintage cars."

Malcolm smote himself on the forehead. "That's where I heard of him! There was a documentary about him. He travelled all over the world buying beautiful old cars from potentates who had fallen on hard times. Quite a character."

"He was, indeed." Brian smiled. "On a sunny day you could often seeing him driving around the countryside in an ancient open-topped Daimler. Eccentric as hell, but I liked him. And I shared his obsession, of course. He did nearly all the restoration work himself. But now and again he'd come across a problem he couldn't solve or couldn't source the parts for and then he came to us."

"Who's us?" Laura asked.

"Sorry, I should have said. "Wetherby's – the garage I work for – *worked* for," he corrected himself. "Every so often he'd ask them to send someone to give him a hand. And they usually sent me." He smiled modestly. "I am really good with old cars. I have a feel for them. And I care. I cared that they were restored properly with authentic parts. Sometimes I had to make the parts myself. That's how I knew there would be no plastic in any car older than 1910."

"And you just stole one?" Laura was shocked.

"Well, he was dead," said Brian, with a rueful smile. "The cars would have been sold off the highest bidder. Would already have been sold if he hadn't died intestate. About a million distant relatives came out of the woodwork and made claims on the estate, so the house was just locked up while the lawyers tried to sort it out. And anyway," he went on, "I think he'd have liked me to have it. He'd know at least one of his babies would be properly looked after. And besides, it was a matter of life and death."

"Yes, of course," said Laura, feeling slightly ashamed of her stuffy reaction. After all, it was *Chloe's* life he was saving.

"So I fixed up my car well enough to get us there and we packed it with everything we thought would be useful for us, and maybe you, too." He held up his hands. "Nothing plastic, I promise. And we drove over to Piers' place, broke into the garage and swapped our car for the beauty outside."

23. Piers Bentley-More's Garage

Chloe had found the journey to Piers' house very disturbing. The streets were deserted. Shops were closed and shuttered, office buildings stood dark and unoccupied. The commercial districts felt dead and abandoned.

But the residential areas were worse. There were no people, only abandoned cars lining the pavements on either side.

"And then I saw a curtain twitch and I realised there *were* people. Inside all those houses there were people, living on whatever food they had managed to hoard, some of them dying of COVID, some of them maybe dead already, beginning to decay. I began to imagine I could smell them."

"You didn't imagine it," Brian said.

Chloe shuddered. " It was really creepy. All those people watching us. Watching us drive past. Maybe hating us because we had a car that worked and we were getting away."

It was a relief to get out into the countryside but the feeling of being watched persisted. Chloe gave a little cry of relief when the manor house came into view.

The front gates were chained and padlocked, but Brian drove on past, following the containing wall in a sweeping circle, until, at last, they came to a break with a wooden gate.

Brian smiled. "I thought they wouldn't bother to padlock this one," he said, pulling up in front of the gate.

Chloe got out of the car, looking around her, half-expecting someone to be lurking in the bushes, ready to ambush them.

"It'll be OK," Brian said. "Nobody's going to come out here. Just open the gate and I'll drive through."

Not entirely reassured, Chloe did as she was told, closing the gate behind her as soon as the car had passed and jumping back in.

The road, if you could call it that, was a dirt track leading, not to the house, but to a massive building the size of an aircraft hangar. There was a chain and padlock on the big double doors.

"Bugger!" said Brian. "What did they do that for? There's a perfectly good lock."

He got out and went round the back of the car to retrieve a screwdriver from his toolbox.

Chloe got out and stared at the building in front of her. So this was Piers Bentley-More's garage? It was about ten times the size of the biggest house Chloe had ever lived in.

Some distance away, at the top of a hill, stood the manor house itself, a rambling building, surrounded by outhouses and stables. She didn't know much about architecture but it looked old. It also seemed to be in a state of some disrepair. Some of the shutters hung drunkenly at the wrong angles and there were bald patches on the roof where tiles were broken or missing.

Not so the garage. It presented a spanking new façade. Sir Piers Bentley-More clearly cared more for his garage than his house.

Brian unscrewed the hasp and both padlock and chain dropped to one side.

"I never would have thought of doing that!" Chloe was torn between shock and admiration.

"Easier than breaking the padlock," he said, winking at her. "Bit of a design fault there."

Chloe gave him an uncertain smile and looked around nervously. Surely someone, somewhere, would see them acting suspiciously and call the police?

"No chance," said Brian. "How are they going to phone them? And how could the police get here without transport?"

Then he took a key from his pocket inserted it in the lock, and pushed open one of the doors.

"You've got a key?"

"Piers gave me one ages ago," he said. "I'd sometimes be working here for a couple of weeks at a time. I even slept here sometimes."

Chloe shivered, thinking of him sleeping alone in that soulless structure, then followed him in. Brian clicked a switch on the wall and the space was instantly flooded with light. Choe looked up in amazement at a bank of powerful halogen bulbs in the ceiling.

"Solar," he said. "We fitted it three years ago."

She followed him into the building, glancing up at the lights as she went, not quite able to believe they were real.

The garage was full of old cars.

·"This was Piers' latest project." Brian indicated an ancient wreck of a car in the centre of the floor. He stroked the bonnet affectionately. "A 1912 Wolseley Landaulette. Lovely old girl. We were waiting for some parts for her. She would have been really something special when we restored her." He shook his head sadly. "Never happen now."

Abruptly his mood changed and he smiled at her. "Why don't you get out the hamper and sort out a picnic while I prospect for our new transport? The flat's up there." He indicated a staircase in one corner.

Chloe raised her eyebrows.

"Well, when he was working here he needed somewhere to wash and eat and so on."

The flat was better equipped than their place in Guildford, consisting of a comfortable living area, bathroom and bedroom and what her mother would have called a 'kitchenette'. Most things in the sixties seemed to end in '-ette', Chloe reflected – leatherette, Dansette, launderette, kitchenette. This one had a hob, an oven, a microwave, a fridge, a kettle and a toaster.

"Go easy on the electric stuff," he shouted. "Don't switch two things on at once."

When she came back down, Brian was standing with his hands on his hips, surveying the collection of cars.

There were some splendid, shiny vehicles standing in ranks to the right of the old wreck, but Brian ignored them and instead went across to the left where a dozen or so rather less impressive cars huddled together as if for comfort.

"What's wrong with the other ones over there?"

Brian looked back at her. "Too new. They'll all have plastic in them. I know these are all right – all before 1910 – and I worked on some of them myself."

She left him to tinker with the cars and went out to get the hamper. She didn't like leaving their own car outside where anybody could see it. So far there was no-one in sight, but who knew? Someone could be alerting the authorities right now,

"Shouldn't we move our car inside?"

Brian shrugged. "OK," he said. "Best not to take any chances." He stood up, wiped his hands on his (cotton) trousers and went out to fetch the car.

Once it was inside, Chloe breathed a sigh of relief and took the hamper up to the flat. For a horrible moment she thought they'd forgotten the tin-opener, but there it was, stuck between a tin of potatoes and a jar of mayonnaise. By the time she'd assembled the food, Brian had selected their transport. "Ford Model T," he said, leaning on the door jamb and smiling at her. "Known as the Tin

Lizzie. Very reliable for its time. Proper workhorse. Plenty of capacity for spare petrol cans and luggage. It's even got a roof-rack."

After they'd eaten, Chloe cleared away the tins and put the plates and cutlery in the sink. To her amazement, the water ran hot. She switched the tap off quickly, afraid she'd use up the solar.

"Don't worry," Brian said. "Separate system."

She washed up, revelling in the hot water. For weeks they'd had to heat all their water in a pan on the camping stove. Having hot water straight from the tap felt like an unbelievable luxury – almost magical. She dried the washing up and packed it back in the hamper, careful to remember the tin-opener. Then she hesitated. No point in putting the hamper back in their own car.

Brian was busy working on the Tin Lizzie,

"Is there anything I can do?" she asked.

"Won't be a sec," he said. "Just checking her vital fluids. Then we can run her. You can fetch those bricks if you like."

He indicated a small pile of bricks near the door. Mystified, Chloe carried them over, two at a time.

"Just pop one under each wheel," he said.

Why? Didn't it have any brakes? She didn't fancy driving all the way to the cottage with no brakes.

"It's just she has a tendency to walk when you're cranking the starter," he said, taking a starting handle out of the boot and attaching it to the bonnet.

"My God," muttered Chloe. "It's like Hastings' car in Poirot."

Brian grinned at her over his shoulder then bent to crank the engine. It fired after a couple of turns. "What a beauty!" he said, climbing into the driver's seat. "Right, chocks away."

Laura removed the bricks and the car drove sedately through the big double doors and into the yard.

A few minutes later he backed it into the garage again, brought it to rest beside his own car and cut the engine.

"Right, now we can transfer all our worldly goods."

Chloe felt excited now, and anxious to be off.

As she picked up the hamper, he stopped her. "No, leave that out for supper."

"What? Aren't we going straight away?"

Brian laughed.

"Not in this car," he said. "No lights. It'll take about nine hours to get there, so we'll have to wait till daylight. We don't want to have to sleep in the car."

"What are those?" Chloe asked, swallowing her disappointment and pointing at what were clearly two headlamps at the front of the car.

"Oil lamps. They're there so people can see you coming but useless for seeing where you're going."

"Oh," said Chloe in a small voice.

"Darling," he said, "We can be off at first light and in the meantime we can spend a pleasant evening watching television and then sleep in a proper bed.

Chloe looked at him as if he were mad.

"Recorded stuff. There's a hard drive connected to the TV."

Later, in the comfortable bed, she murmured, "Why don't we just stay here?"

He kissed her on the nose. "Because, my sweet, this isn't a farm. It could be made into one, but not in time to support us now. We'd have to take risks, going out for supplies, meeting people who might not be friendly. And anyway, it would be much better to be in a community. If your friends will take us in, we'll have a ready-made community, already set up to be self-sufficient. If they won't, we may well come back here. But I'd rather try them first."

~*~

"Right! Here we go!"

The Tin Lizzie pulled away from the gate and sailed off, heading for the motorway. Chloe glanced back at Piers' garage as it fell out of sight. There was nothing to show anyone had been there. The padlock was back on the door, the wooden gate was closed. At some future date, should anyone investigate, they might be puzzled by the presence of one modern car amongst the museum pieces, but Brian thought it unlikely that anyone would investigate. Not for a long time, anyway. And anyone investigating would be likely to be interested in its potential for farming, rather than the commercial value of a collection of old cars.

It was only now, driving along at a ponderous forty miles an hour ("Forty-five's her absolute maximum," Brian said) that she realised just how devastating the disaster was. They saw nobody, nobody at all, in the whole nine hour, 360 mile journey. The motorway stretched, utterly empty, for mile after mile. Occasionally they saw an abandoned car on the hard shoulder or on one of the slip roads. Other than that there was nothing, just miles of three lane carriageway and signs that very few people would ever read again.

"It can't be all over, surely? Somebody will come and sort it out:"

"I don't see how," Brian said. "We would have survived the virus, I'm sure. They would have found a vaccine that worked. They would have suffered a short economic depression and then taken up the old life again. But this –" he waved his hand at the empty land on either side. "This is terminal."

~*~

The little group sitting round the table was silent for a few minutes.

"Do you mean to say that just about everyone is dying?" Malcolm said at last.

"Well, I don't *know* that," Brian said. "We didn't have enough information before the communications went down."

"It's unlikely that everyone would die," said Jonathan. "No plague in history killed a hundred percent of the population. You have to assume that a reasonable percentage would be naturally immune. And there will be people in the countryside who never had any contact with this new strain. It may burn itself out without them ever even knowing about it."

Nobody said anything else. Malcolm was thinking that this probably meant there would be no marauding hordes. *Johnathan would be safe!* He had an instant's memory of Jonathan, lying half on the pavement and half in the gutter, his beautiful face bruised and swollen, blood in his hair – the sound of retreating footsteps and a shout of, "Serves you right, you black pansy." *Never again!* If anyone threatened Jonathan he would kill them without a second thought. He would have beaten off the marauding hordes with his bare hands.

He shook his head, shocked at his own reaction of relief at the thousands of deaths which had made Jonathan safer. When he spoke, he just sounded tired. "So we really are on our own, then."

Gary was stunned into silence, thinking it must be like this all over the world, each country had too much on its plate handling its own catastrophe to reach out and help another. The rich countries failing as the plastic plague brought down all their sophisticated systems – the poor ones with less reliance on those systems but also no means of combatting the virus.

Laura sat, white-faced, thinking, not of marauding hordes or global catastrophe, but of her parents, even now perhaps struggling with the virus, unable to breathe and with no-one to help.

24. Homecoming

Laura was in the henhouse collecting eggs when a bell rang. She stood up in alarm, knocking her head on the beam above, the basket of eggs swaying dangerously on her arm, as she tottered before regaining her balance. She came out of the hen house just as Auntie Martha came running past her across the courtyard towards the gate.

"They're here!" she shouted as she ran.

Laura put her hand on her stomach in an instinctively protective gesture and stared after her. She had a surprising turn of speed for a nonagenarian.

~*~

The boys had spent a good part of the spring and summer putting in defensive measures. The first was an alarm wire along the whole of the fence round the twin farms, with cameras at strategic points. If necessary, parts of the fence could be electrified to keep off unwanted visitors. And, yes, it turned out Jonathan *had* provided weapons but only (he hoped) to use as a deterrent. None of them were sure they could actually shoot anyone. Except Malcolm. He knew he could shoot anyone who threatened Jonathan.

Now someone had disturbed the wire. And it had to be a person, not an animal. The wire was too high up to be triggered by anything smaller than a cow or a horse, (either of which they would have welcomed). Auntie Martha must have seen who it was on the camera. Laura put down the basket and went after her, not running – she was too big to do more than a clumsy jog. The baby bounced in her belly and she slowed down to more sensible walk.

Malcolm passed them on the way, driving the Land Rover. He parked at the gate and dismounted, holding his rifle at the ready. There were two people on the other side. Beggars by the looks of them. Half-starved and dressed in rags.

"It's me," the woman said. "Dora."

He stared, hardly able to believe that these pitiful creatures could possibly be the people he knew.

"Jesus," he said, dropping the rifle and going to open the gate.

He was about to go to them when he remembered. "The plague," he said. "Are you OK?"

Ken said nothing. He looked utterly exhausted.

"We're safe," Dora said in a cracked whisper. "Haven't seen anyone else for months. No plastic." She gave a not quite sane laugh. Ken keeled over on his back and Malcolm went to help him up, just as Auntie Martha arrived, out of breath (but not unduly so, considering her age).

Between them, they managed to get Ken and Dora into the Land Rover. Auntie Martha couldn't believe how little they weighed. *My God, when did they last eat?*

Malcolm picked up the rifle and got back in the car.

Halfway up the drive they picked up Laura, who stared open-mouthed at her parents and then burst into tears.

In the kitchen they found Gary and Chloe busy making cheese sandwiches. Gary fetched two over, with the clear intention of giving them to Ken and Dora.

"Don't give them that!" Auntie Martha snapped and Gary halted, baffled. "But there's plenty," he said. "Laura baked yesterday."

"Oh you silly boy," said Auntie Martha. "I don't *grudge* them the bread. It's dangerous to give famine victims anything too substantial. Laura, make some tea. I'll make a broth for them."

"How does she know this stuff?" Malcolm asked.

"Laura's grandad was one of those who liberated Belsen," Auntie Martha said over her shoulder. "There were people there in an even worse state than these two, if you can believe that. The soldiers did the obvious thing. They fed them. And a lot of them died. Their systems couldn't take it. They killed them with kindness. Rupert was horrified. I don't intend to do the same to his child."

Laura made the tea, hardly taking her eyes off her parents, who were sitting side by side, holding hands. Dora was smiling, but Ken appeared to be falling asleep.

"Put sugar in it," Auntie Martha said.

"My mum doesn't take sugar," Laura objected.

"She does today," said Auntie Martha, in a voice that would brook no disobedience.

Dora took her mug gingerly and sipped at it. Ken waved his away.

"Dad, please drink it. It'll do you good," Laura begged, but he just laid his head back and ignored her.

Just then, Ben, Jonathan and Brian arrived with both dogs in tow and everyone stepped in to prevent the dogs from jumping up at the new arrivals.

Ben picked up Ken's mug of tea and tried to persuade him to drink it. "I don't want it," Ken said. "I just want to sleep. Go away."

"Leave him be," said Auntie Martha. "Just make sure he has some broth when it's ready."

"I'm afraid if he goes to sleep he won't wake up," said Laura.

"He got this far," said Auntie Martha. "He's not going to give up now."

But Laura wasn't so sure. She thought he might have been driven by the desire to get Dora to a safe place and now he'd done that he might just let go. She'd never seen him so dispirited.

When the broth arrived, Dora took hers obediently, but Ken refused again.

"Please, Daddy," Laura said.

"No, I won't drink it."

"Yes you bloody well will, my boy," said Ben, sitting beside him and feeding him like a child. Ken turned his head away and Ben gently turned it back towards him and spooned some broth into his mouth. Ken spluttered and it ran down his chin. Ben caught it expertly and shovelled it back in his mouth. After a brief struggle, Ken gave in and allowed himself to be fed.

"He's really good at this," Gary said. "You'd never think he'd never had children."

"Ah, but he did," said Laura. "He had my mum when she was little, and then he had me. He was great with me. Used to take me for walks and tell me all the names of the trees and the flowers and the birds."

"And the butterflies?"

Laura gave Gary her special smile. "Yes, and the butterflies."

Gary hugged her. "It's going to be all right," he whispered into her hair.

"I know," she said, and wept a little, very quietly, against his chest. Then she went to sit next to her mother and helped her finish off her broth.

"Come on, Chloe," said Auntie Martha. "Let's go and make up the spare room."

"Isn't that the last one, now?" Chloe asked, as they went up the stairs. "We must be running out of accommodation."

"Well, it's the last one in the cottage," said Auntie Martha. "But there's still Gary's studio. And Ben's got two spare rooms and a baby room."

We may have to move over to Ben's when the baby comes, Chloe thought, thinking of the tiny embryo, no bigger than a fingernail, curled up in her own womb.

25. Ken and Dora

It had been perfect summer – long, hot days, warm nights. This was how Laura remembered her childhood summers at the cottage. Had they really all been like that, or was it a product of nostalgia rather than a true memory? The last few years had certainly been different – unpredictable warm spells, freezing winters and flooding in the lowlands. If course they had no idea what was happening in the lowlands this year. There could be fire, floods and famine for all she knew – certainly plague. Their last news from the outside world had arrived with her parents a few weeks ago.

Not that Ken and Dora had known much more about the whole picture than Chloe and Brian had.

~*~

After that last, abruptly terminated phone call, Ken and Dora had decided to wait it out. They had food to last them for some considerable time. And they were particularly fortunate in the clothing department. Ken's habit of bringing back mementoes from all over the world had left them with a variety of garments in natural fibres – hand-made, most of them. They might not be fashionable, but they were serviceable.

Ken was more concerned about their stocks of fuel. They'd had a coal delivery just a couple of weeks before the lockdown but he wasn't confident it would be enough to see them through to the warmer weather. The gas was still working, but for how long? He began to worry about how vulnerable his coal-shed was.

He used to like most of his neighbours. Now he had the feeling they were enemies, waiting their chance to steal anything they could.

He checked the car (under the watchful eyes of his neighbours – he saw curtains twitch in several windows).

He daren't attempt to start the engine. If it worked he had a strong suspicion the car would be stolen during the night. For the first time he regretted not getting a bigger house with a garage.

Deliberately, he turned the starter without pulling out the throttle and let it whine a few times before getting out of the car and holding his hands up in a gesture of defeat. (The curtains twitched back into place).

Could they sneak out and steal a car further away from the estate? He dismissed the idea immediately. No-one was going to leave a working car unattended out in the open. He settled for sneaking out late at night and spraying the car electrics with disinfectant. It worked on the phones and the computers (both now useless, of course). It should work on the car. Other than that, he saw no course but to wait it out and look for an opportunity.

The estate was now regularly patrolled by police and occasionally by soldiers. What were they expecting? A full-scale insurrection? It seemed unlikely when most people didn't even have any reasonable clothes to wear. The few who appeared on the street were dressed in bizarre outfits, cobbled together from whatever material they possessed which had survived the plastic plague. He averted his gaze from the truly horrific aspect of Mrs Brigham from the corner shop shuffling down the street in what appeared to be a tent made from uncut moquette.

The police and the military appeared to still have viable clothing but close inspection revealed a few anomalies. They all looked a bit old-fashioned, as if they'd found an arcane Army and Navy Store that still had supplies from the last war. Or whatever the police equivalent was. The soldiers were wearing tin hats and the policemen were dressed like Dixon of Dock Green, with pointed helmets. Did they still wear those? He had the impression that policemen these days wore peaked hats, like traffic wardens, and yellow jackets - or were they gilets? Not these woollen jackets with brass buttons, surely?

One morning he woke up in the small hours to see dark figures bringing out bundles from the house opposite. The house belonged to Mr Denham, not a close friend but Ken was on greeting terms with him. He was a nice enough chap who worked for the council. Married with two children.

It was difficult to see what was going on. There were no street lights (obviously) and the men were working by torchlight. He watched as they fetched out two large and two smaller bundles. There was a muffled expletive as one of the men fumbled and almost dropped his end of the package. Ken watched in disbelief as the torch beam caught on the hand that had flopped out. He looked away, feeling sick.

They were caught in a slowly closing trap. Unable to leave the house. And now he knew for sure that the virus that he had treated so lightly had reached their estate. It was in their street, in the house opposite. How many of the other houses had plague victims dying inside? Perhaps the lack of clothing was not the only reason there were so few people on the streets.

He knew that a new strain of the virus had emerged just before Christmas and it was supposed to be more virulent. What did that mean? That it spread more quickly, certainly, but was it also more dangerous, more likely to kill? The government had announced that there was no reason to think so, but it was too soon to know. They also said there was no reason to suppose that it would not respond to the new vaccine that was being rolled out. That's what they called it – *rolled out* – as if it were a piece of pastry. Irrelevant now, of course. The vaccine had to be kept at very low temperatures and there was no power. No means of transporting it even if they could keep it cool.

And what about the health services? It didn't take a genius to work out that with no power, no communications and no viable transport the hospitals must be unable to cope. It stood to reason that people must be dying in their own homes, waiting for the faceless men to come in the dead of the night and remove them – to what? Mass graves? They did that in Italy, didn't they? In the first wave of the virus. He'd seen footage of the lorries arriving in the middle of night. The men, soldiers probably, loading the bodies inside and taking them away. There were no lorries here. The soldiers might still have uniforms but he hadn't seen a moving vehicle since early January.

He realised with a shock that he had lost track of the days. He wasn't even sure what month it was.

The next day he stacked all the parlour furniture against the wall and took up the carpet. That night, he emptied the coal-shed, as quietly as he could. Taking it by the wheelbarrow load and emptying it onto the parlour floor. Dora wept at the desecration, but did not protest. The next day Ken took the very last pieces of coal out of the shed, making sure that a few curtains were twitching, then left the coal-shed door wide open – a clear indication that it was empty and not worth investigating.

If only he'd been better prepared, he'd have put in an alarm system. Of course, if he'd taken it seriously in the first place he wouldn't have had to prepare at all. Just get Dora and all their important possessions in the car and drive to Cumbria before the trap was even set.

A few days later Smokey didn't come home. She was Dora's cat, really, but she was a sweet little thing and he was fond of her. Nevertheless he wasn't prepared to leave the house to look for her. He had a fairly good idea of what might have happened to her and he didn't believe he had any chance of finding her. He tried to comfort Dora with the usual platitudes, saying she'd come home when she was hungry. But Dora wasn't a woman who could be lulled easily. "I know she's not coming home, Ken," she said, wiping her eyes on a dishcloth (they'd run out of tissues long ago). "I just hope she didn't suffer."

It was time to go.

They packed their hiking rucksacks with food.

"We're going to need clean underwear," Dora said.

"Just one change," Ken said. "And wear as many clothes as you can. They won't mind if we're a bit smelly when we turn up. They'll just be glad we made it."

They put the rucksacks by the back door and waited for a break in the weather.

"First dry day," Ken said. "We'll go as soon as it gets dark."

It rained steadily for two weeks. Now even the police had disappeared.

Then the sun broke through. They ate a hearty breakfast and a rather less hearty meal in the afternoon. Apprehension had spoilt their appetites. The police were in the streets again. Checking the houses. Occasionally trying a door. Nobody else appeared.

"My mother used to say," Dora mused, " that if ever you were in trouble, find a policeman."

Ken laughed humourlessly.

As soon as the sun went down, they donned thick sheepskin jackets over a motley assortment of garments, strapped on their walking boots, helped each other on with their rucksacks and quietly opened the back door. No curtains twitched. Silently, they crept through the back garden and out into the fields behind the house, At the top of the hill they stopped in the shadow of a small copse of trees and looked back down at their home of forty years. A long time ago now, it seemed, Ken had told his daughter it would be a wrench to leave this place. He found it wasn't the wrench he had imagined it would be.

They hitched up their rucksacks and carried on.

Five minutes later they heard gunfire coming from below and exchanged a terrified glance-

"Shit," said Ken. "Only just in time!"

~*~

It had taken them an interminable time to get to Cumbria. They had eaten sparingly. When they came across an inhabited place they waited till dark to get past it. When their food ran out they had to forage for anything edible. Dora was grateful for her childhood tuition from Ben in the wild things growing near the twin farms. She didn't know every single plant, but she could distinguish some of the edible mushrooms. There were acorns in the forests and occasional fruit trees, sometimes with a few of last year's wizened apples or plums, but they could never find enough to stave off their hunger. Once they found an abandoned farmhouse with a stock of tinned food in the larder and they holed up there for two weeks until there was just enough food left to refill the rucksacks. Once Dora tripped over a root and sprained her ankle and they rested up in a shepherd's hut for several days while Ken scoured the surrounding hills for edible roots and mushrooms.

All in all it took them more than two months for a journey that used to take two and a half hours. And in all that time they saw less than a dozen people. Those they saw were at a distance, in ones or twos, mostly working on the land. They avoided the towns but when the wind was in the wrong direction they could smell them.

But they had made it!

~*~

From the back courtyard Laura could just see the rest of the family, including her mum and dad, working in the lower field, binding sheaves. *Only reapers, reaping early In among the bearded barley.* Where did that come from? Was it The Lady of Shalott? Except *her* family was reaping wheat, not barley. All of them, except for her and Auntie Martha.

Laura was exempt because her baby was due any day now (she thought – it was something of a guess) and Auntie Martha on account of her great age (although, judging by how fast she ran down the drive the day Ken and Dora turned up, she was fitter than any of them).

Her mum and dad were now completely recovered from their ordeal. If anything they were a little more portly than before. They joined in enthusiastically with the harvest, glad to be useful. Glad to be alive.

And Laura was glad to be alive as well. She felt her baby kicking in her womb and told her to calm down. If it was a girl (she was sure it was a girl. Auntie Martha was seldom wrong) they were going to call her Grace. They'd wanted to call her Martha, but Auntie Martha had vetoed the idea. "One Martha is quite enough," she said. " If you want to call her after somebody, why don't you call her Violet, after your grandmother? If my child had lived," she mused, "I was going to call her Grace. After my wonderful great aunt, who left me this cottage. If it hadn't been for her we might not be here now."

Laura and Gary stared at her, amazed at this sudden revelation of Auntie Martha's secret past.

"I didn't know you'd had a baby," said Laura.

"I didn't." Auntie Martha snapped. "Not really."

It didn't seem to be the sort of response that invited further questions.

Laura decided to ask her mother later. Strangely, just having her mother here had dispelled all her fears about the birth. She felt full of energy and ready to get on with it.

26. Three Years Later

It was a beautiful summer's day. The harvest was weeks away and there was so little to do that the family had declared a holiday. The men were all down by the river bank, ostensibly fishing, but mainly just lazing about. Auntie Martha and Dora, neither of whom had the slightest interest in fishing, (or, in the case of Dora, fish) were doing some desultory weeding in the vegetable garden and making plans for the next plantings. Chloe, Laura and the children were in the front garden.

Three year old Grace and Chloe's twins were playing in the playpen, watched over by Bernie. The twins had been a surprise to everyone. Neither Chloe nor Brian had a history of twins in their family as far as they knew. The boys were identical – Gordon and Robert (although everyone just referred to them as 'the twins', as if they had no separate identity). Grace bullied them mercilessly, taking advantage of her five month superiority, but the twins were oblivious to her attempts at domination. They spoke to each other in a gibberish that sounded just on the edge of comprehensibility. Jonathan was fascinated by them and listened for hours trying to grasp the import of their arcane pronunciations.

The playpen had been constructed by Ken, who had discovered the woodworking tools, which Jonathan had thoughtfully provided as part of his stock of equipment, with a joy that seemed out of all proportion to everyone except Brian (who understood about obsession). The first thing he had made was cot for Chloe's baby, quickly duplicated when it transpired there were two babies instead of the expected one. (Grace had already inherited the family cot). Since then, he had gone on to produce an abundance of baby equipment and toys, finding just as much satisfaction in making full-size artefacts as he had in the dolls' house furniture he had been producing for years.

Laura was painting; her easel set up next to the playpen – Violet, the new baby, in a basket beside her. Chloe was unashamedly asleep on the lawn, her book neglected beside her on the grass.

So when the bell rang, nobody heard it.

"Well, here's a scene of rustic bliss."

Laura spun round to face the owner of the voice. Chloe woke instantly and sprang to her feet.

Both women moved to stand between the visitor and the babies – tigresses defending their cubs.

"It's me, Laura. John – John Evans." The visitor took off his hat, which had been shading his face.

"Good God, John, what on earth are *you* doing here?" She couldn't keep the accusatory tone out of her voice. "You frightened me."

"I am the bearer of news," he said, replacing the hat – a disreputable old straw sunhat of the kind worn by donkeys. "Glad tidings, I hope."

Chloe looked from one to the other in confusion.

At that moment Auntie Martha came round the corner, accompanied by Dora, both carrying trowels and baskets of weeds.

"John Evans," she exclaimed. "As I live and breathe."

"And very glad I am that you do," he replied, doffing his hat again in a flamboyant manner, reminiscent of Regency farces. "How is Ben these days?"

"Fishing – ostensibly," said Auntie Martha, with just a touch of disapproval, as if fishing were somehow immoral or indecent.

"John," said Dora. "It's good to see you. How has it been going?"

"Good, good," said John, pulling up a garden chair and sitting down. "We think the worst is over. The village has survived, more or less intact." He turned to Auntie Martha. "Due, I am reliably informed, to you."

Auntie Martha looked up at the sun. "The men will be back soon, wanting their dinner," she said. "Why don't you join us? Just a salad. It's too hot for a cooked meal."

"What do you mean, the worst is over?" Laura asked. "Do you mean the virus? And what about the plastic plague?"

"We think they've both burned themselves out. We can't be sure but we've seen nothing of either now for months. I wanted to talk to Jonathan about it. He's probably got a better idea than we have. I know he did a lot of information gathering before we lost the internet."

Laura shot an accusing glance at Auntie Martha. How did John know about Jonathan's investigations? Auntie Martha assumed an exaggerated expression of innocence.

"I'll put the kettle on," she said. "I'm sure we could all do with a nice cup of tea."

~*~

The village had survived the crisis. Following Laura's call about isolating the Twin Farms when the first wave had hit Britain, Joe at the George and Dragon had organised a strict lockdown. "We understand about plagues in these parts," he said, thinking of the dreadful outbreak of foot and mouth disease some years before.

It had been relatively easy, since almost all the villagers were farmers or retired and there were very few who needed to travel outside the boundaries except to pick up supplies or attend livestock markets. Cruckford was too far from major cities for easy commuting.

Since it was a one street town, it was easy to erect a gate at each end and put up a sign saying 'Quarantine – please wear a mask on entering.' This deterred casual strangers. During the national lockdown, the delivery drivers all wore masks as a matter of course anyway.

When the national lockdown was lifted, the signs remained in place. Joe insisted that anybody who had to leave the village, for whatever reason, should isolate on their return.

"My publisher was not thrilled," said John, "but he was just being difficult. There was never any need to go in person, for goodness' sake. Everything these days, or *those* days, rather, could be done by email or phone."

The plastic problem was a different matter, though. Not everyone took it seriously at first but the disintegration of the phones (which were always the earliest victims, due to constant handling) soon convinced the unbelievers and they managed to suppress the outbreak with a determined course of regular disinfection. The only major casualty was old Mrs Benson, whose house was contaminated, presumably when her niece (equipped with mobile phone) visited her. The fire which burnt down her house a couple of months later was found to be due to exposed electrical wiring.

"Oh, my God," said Laura, clapping her hand to her mouth in horror.

"It's all right. She survived," John said, "and we installed her in one of the summer cottages. But she lost all her goods and chattels, and it was a salutary lesson for the rest of us. Everyone rallied round and gave her stuff to replace what she'd lost."

He broke off and looked up as the arrival of the rest of the family was heralded by a delighted Bessie.

"Well, well, old lass," he said. "You're still with us, I'm pleased to see."

"Good God, man, she's only nine years old," said Ben, coming round the corner, triumphantly wielding a basket full of fish. "She's only just reaching her prime."

"I'd better get the dinner on," said Auntie Martha.

~*~

Cruckford and its farmsteads were better equipped to deal with the loss of power than most places. Most of the houses were equipped with fireplaces and wood-burning stoves. The village was largely self-sufficient in food and there was plenty of firewood to be collected from the surrounding woods. The most important deficiency was in petrol, paraffin, oil and candles for lighting.

"We syphoned off all the petrol in the cars and used it to keep the tractors going for a while, but we've been ploughing with horses and cattle for the last two years. And lighting's been a real problem. We tried making candles from tallow but they stink abominably, so most of us just sit by firelight in the evening. Like in the olden days. Not you, though, I see," John said, looking up with approval at the solar panels covering the roofs of the farm buildings. "But we think the time has come for us to try to find out what was happening in the outside world. We thought there was a good chance that both plagues would have burnt themselves out by now and we might be justified in making a few discreet visits to nearby towns and sniff out the lay of the land. And since I'm the only one with viable transport . . ."

"Your horse and trap," cried Laura, delighted.

"Indeed," said John.

Auntie Martha leant forward. "So what did you find? What *is* happening in the outside world?"

"Not much, I'm afraid," John said. "The towns seem to be abandoned. I didn't care to look inside any of the buildings but I'm pretty sure there was nobody there. Nobody alive, anyway,"

Laura looked at him in horror. "All those people? All dead?"

"Well, I imagine some of them got away. But the plague must have got millions. And then this plastic thing closing everything down. I think most people were trapped in their homes and maybe those that died of the plague were the lucky ones."

Dora shuddered, remembering the gunshots they had heard as they left Selby.

"We think the army may have finished the rest off," Ken said, taking Dora's hand, "at least in Selby."

He related their experience to John, who nodded. "I'm not really surprised," he said. "And, who knows, maybe it was more humane than leaving them to die of the plague." He brightened. "But you got away, and others will have, too." He looked across at Gary and Malcolm. "

I know of at least one," he said. "Do either of you remember a Mr Alan Dale, erstwhile teacher at St Mark's Grammar School?"

27. The Beginning.

Gary and Malcolm exchanged a delighted look.

"The old bugger," said Malcolm.

"Language, Malcolm," said Chloe, looking pointedly at Grace, who was jumping up and down in the playpen, shouting, "Bugger, bugger, bugger."

Laura picked her up and whispered in her ear, "Not a nice word, Grace, Uncle Malcolm's a naughty boy."

Grace laughed and pointed at Malcolm. "Naughty boy!" she shouted.

Gary was full of questions. "How is he? Has he got his family with him? How far away is this place?"

~*~

John had come across Mr Dale in the village of Lower Winstock, near the Forest of Bowland. Some of the small towns and villages he passed had barricades and KEEP OUT signs, but where they didn't, he had reined in his horse and trap and stopped to speak to the inhabitants. Most people seemed anxious for news and were disappointed when he could tell them little they didn't know already. What he found reassuring was that none of them had suffered any cases of either plague for over a year.

But one person who had not been disappointed was Mr Dale of Lower Winstock. "Cruckford, you say? You don't happen to know a Mr Gary Brent, do you? And possibly a Malcolm Abrams?"

~*~

Following Gary's call, Mr Dale had made his own investigations regarding the plastic eating bacteria, come to the same conclusion as Gary and emailed him with extra information. He had considered isolating the school but decided it was impractical. Firstly because he didn't have much sway with the Board of Governors, secondly because most of the boys would, as a matter of course, go home to their families when the time came and he might have no community to defend, and thirdly because the school was not well set-up for being self-sufficient. Its land was mainly devoted to playing fields rather than farming, and would take too much time and work to convert. Consequently, he had thought much as Malcolm and Jonathan had, and looked for a nice self-sufficient farm in a sparsely inhabited area.

Lower Winstock was a tiny village of only a hundred or so inhabitants, surrounded by farmland and forest. He was unable to buy a farm, as such, but he acquired a large cottage with log stoves and more than enough accommodation for his wife and two children, with the possibility of also taking in any boys who could not return to their homes. Some of the parents lived abroad and he suspected (rightly, as it turned out) that if and when the crisis came there would be no time to reunite them with their families.

The cottage had a great deal of land attached, some of which consisted of a vegetable garden, and he spent his free weekends extending it and stocking up on food and essential supplies. When the third lockdown came, he packed his family off to the cottage and volunteered to man the school and look after the three remaining boarders. When communications broke down, he left a message painted on the wall in the senior common room, with the Lower Winstock address, in case any of the boys' families should come looking for them. None of them did.

The villagers were confused and distressed by the disastrous turn of events. They had been hit hard by the COVID 19 virus, being in a popular tourist area, and were fearful of what would happen now it looked like there would be no vaccine and, indeed, no outside help. Mr Dale had immediately volunteered to work on a local committee tasked with keeping the village safe and looking after the inhabitants. Together they had organised Lower Winstock on much the same lines as Joe had organised Cruckford. It had worked out well. They had lost no more people to the virus, although they had not fared so well against the plastic plague, which had taken a firm hold before Mr Dale arrived. It took well over a year of burning and disinfecting before they were confident they had eradicated it but now, it seemed, the worst was over and they could start looking towards the future.

Now, he felt, it was time to find out more about the state of the outside world and perhaps try to get the scattered communities working together in order to make the best of the world they had left. He was, in fact, planning a fact-finding mission himself when, out of the blue, John Evans had arrived.

"I had an interesting conversation with your Mr Dale," John said. "One of the things that was puzzling me was how few people seem to have survived in the towns. You'd think, wouldn't you, that many would have seen what was coming and got out when the going was good. Perhaps not marauding hordes, but a significant number. Why didn't they?"

Mr Dale had spent some considerable time himself wondering how it had been for the people trapped in the towns. "People in the smaller towns could get to the open countryside without too much difficulty, I imagine," he said, "but what about the major cities? How would you get out of London with no transport? And even if there were people ready and willing to supply the city with food, how could it have been managed? With no vehicles, no trains, not even bicycles – since they are also reliant on plastic. The old ways – horse-drawn wagons, canal barges – could have been reinstated in time, but time is just what we didn't have. And the people were weakened and exhausted by years of austerity and a punishing plague. I think many who could have left didn't even try. I think they hid in their homes, waiting for a rescue that was never going to come, and by the time they realised it was never going to come, they were half-starved and unable to summon the strength to go."

The two of them had sat in gloomy silence, contemplating the millions of personal tragedies amongst the world catastrophe which had descended on them.

"I suppose there will be communities like ours all over the land, each struggling with their own problems, some perhaps dealing with refugees from the towns and cities," said Mr Dale. "The reason we have seen none, I imagine, is because our little villages are so remote."

He shook his head. "But look at it this way. The planet is still fertile. The climate may settle back to its previous stability now we are no longer burning fossil fuels. And we are an ingenious species. I think those of us who are left will get together and rebuild a better society." He rubbed his hands. "Time to get to work."

~*~

Jonathan was less positive than John had hoped about the end of the plagues.

"Statistically, they can only be eradicated by vaccination," he said. "Take the bubonic plague, for instance. There was a major epidemic in Europe in the 14th century but outbreaks of it recurred regularly right up to the 17th century, when it finally appeared to die down. But it's still not completely dead. It still occurs from time to time in some parts of the world. This scotches Johnson's belief in herd immunity. What seems to happen is, without a viable vaccine, the plague dies down either because it mutates to a less deadly variety, which is what we think happened with the 'Spanish' flu of 1918, or a certain immunity builds up but the plague recurs as the population expands and new people are exposed to it."

"Shit," said Malcolm, ignoring Chloe's disapproving look. "So without a vaccine, we're buggered."

"Not necessarily," Jonathan said. "It might not return for years or never at all. We just don't know enough about it. The plastic plague, however, is more problematical. It's bacterial and bacteria are virtually indestructible. They can lie dormant for unknown eons of time and then revive when the conditions are right. That's why it's so dangerous to let the Arctic ice melt. God knows what it might uncover. If you ask me, what we should be concentrating on is rebuilding our society without using plastic at all."

"Can we?" Malcolm asked, thinking of all the technology that depended on it.

"We can try, can't we? There's nearly always an organic alternative. But it's going to take a lot of work and a lot of research. Meanwhile, we disinfect those things that are really important to us and lead a simpler life."

A general air of gloom settled on the company.

"Well, I don't know about you," said Auntie Martha, "but I've been living a simple life for nigh on a hundred years and never felt any lack. Look on the bright side. We've all been expecting something much worse than this. We thought the world was coming to an end. I'll go and put the kettle on."

"I've never been happier in my life than I have these last few years," said Ben. "Ever since the lads moved in. It's like they're the sons I never had."

Jonathan moved across and put his arm around Ben's shoulder. "You find your family as you go through life," he said. "To all intents and purposes we *are* your sons."

After a moment's hesitation, Malcolm came and sat at Ben's other side. "Couldn't agree more," he said, "Dad."

Ben felt his throat constrict with emotion, and gave a little cough to cover his embarrassment. "Frog in the throat," he said, wiping an arm across his eyes.

Everyone laughed and the gloom lifted – just like that!

Brian leant over to speak to John Evans. "Did you say the main problem for the village is petrol?"

John nodded.

"Well, I can sort that out. I worked in a garage for years. I know how to break into petrol stores. Fancy coming on an expedition with me?"

"I've been thinking," Gary said to Jonathan. "The virus doesn't last on surfaces for very long, does it?"

"Usually no more than five days."

"And the plastic plague? How long does it take before things start falling apart?"

"Well, there's been no proper research, but it's clearly fairly rapid. Once infected I got the impression it took days, maybe a few weeks at most."

"So, if we were to break into a store or warehouse and everything was intact, could we be confident that it was safe?"

Jonathan grinned at him. "You've got a point there, young Brent. Go to the top of the class. We could investigate the more far-flung commercial estates and warehouse districts and see what we can pick up."

"Solar stuff, first. Let's see if our favourite supplier is still intact," Malcolm said, getting excited now. "We could fit out the whole village with electricity." He turned to John. "Do the lads still live there – the ones who helped me sort this place out?"

"Oh yes," said John. "They're doing handyman stuff now, and helping out with farm work."

"And Mr Dale's village," Gary said. "We could sort them out too."

By the time Auntie Martha returned with the tea things, they were all in animated discussion.

"Disposable nappies," murmured Laura. "What joy!"

Auntie Martha gave her a hard look. "And where, exactly, were you thinking of disposing of them?"

Laura sighed. She was right, of course. They shouldn't even consider going back to their old throw-away society ways. For a moment she pined for an easier time when they didn't know that just about everything they did was destroying the planet, then she brightened as she remembered the horrible old copper boiler and her lovely new washing machine.

"Quite right, Auntie Martha," she said, and got up to help with the tea things and the lunch.

Looking round the table later at the happy crowd tucking into salad and crusty bread, she realised that she had everything she'd ever wanted right here. They were one big family. Only she and her parents were actually related, but they were a family, nevertheless. And the village people, too. John Evans and Joe, Dr Wilson and Mrs Jessop from the corner shop. The farming folk in the scattered homesteads, and Gary's beloved Mr Dale, whom she might finally meet at last.

One big family, working together to put the world to rights.

Bernie came and put his head on her knee.

God was in his heaven and all was right with the world.

THE END

ABOUT THE STORY

I was sitting with my two dearest friends, Caroline and Billy, and Caroline said, "You know that bacteria they've invented that eats plastic? What if it escaped?"

That was the last time I saw Caroline and Billy in person, before Coronavirus, before lockdown.

An awful lot has happened since then, and I have spent much of the intervening time on the internet, like Laura in the story, campaigning for a better world. But in between I researched the implications of Caroline's chance observation. And they horrified me.

So here goes. A possible answer to Caroline's question. This might be what would happen if the plastic-eating enzyme escaped.

When I started writing the story no-one had heard of Coronavirus, but the advent of the pandemic made me realise how much more devasting the plastic plague would be if it happened at the same time. So I rooted the story firmly against a background of actual events right up to the point where the phones begin to melt. The rest is entirely my own invention.

ABOUT THE AUTHOR

Jenny Twist was born in York and brought up in the West Yorkshire mill town of Heckmondwike, the eldest grandchild of a huge extended family.

She left school at fifteen and went to work in an asbestos factory. After working in various jobs, including bacon-packer and escapologist's assistant (she was The Lovely Tanya), she returned to full-time education and did a BA in history, at Manchester, and post-graduate studies at Oxford.

She stayed in Oxford working as a recruitment consultant for many years and it was there that she met and married her husband, Vic.

In 2001 they retired and moved to Southern Spain where they live with their rather eccentric dogs and cat. Besides writing, she enjoys reading, knitting and attempting to do fiendishly difficult logic puzzles. Since moving to Spain she has written four novels and numerous short stories.

In July 2018 she was awarded the coveted TOP FEMALE AUTHOR award in Fantasy/Horror/Paranormal/Science Fiction by The Authors Show

You can find all my books on Amazon.
author.to/JennyTwist

Visit me on my Facebook page. I love talking to my readers.

https://www.facebook.com/pages/Jenny-Twist-Author/291166404240446

Or you can follow me on my website: https://sites.google.com/site/jennytwistauthor/home

Amazon Author Page
author.to/JennyTwist

Goodreads Author Page
http://www.goodreads.com/author/show/4848320.Jenny_Twist

You can contact me any time on casahoya@gmail.com or you could leave a review on Amazon or Goodreads. I am always really grateful for reviews.

If you enjoyed this story, you might like to read my collection of short political satires. Here's an excerpt from 'Hidden Agenda': -

Excerpt – Hidden Agenda

It wasn't the hospital's fault. They were short-staffed and the maternity unit was busier than usual. Anyway, the baby *looked* perfectly normal. Apart from a slight silvery sheen to his skin and something a little bit odd about the eyes, he was no different from the other babies born that day.

A bell rang further down the corridor and the nurse, who had been staring at the baby (which was, disturbingly, staring back) shook herself, went to answer the bell and forgot all about the very uncomfortable feeling the encounter had given her.

Nobody noticed the tall, dark man, who walked down the corridor, carrying a small bundle. In a few easy strides he reached the front door and stepped outside.

As he climbed into the black, shiny car waiting at the curb, he was laughing.

~ * ~

"Colin, don't plug that in there!"
Colin plugged it in.

There was an almighty crack, a vivid flash, a smell of burning plastic and all the lights went out.

"What the fuckin' hell do you think you're doing, you moron?"

Colin was hunched over the socket, staring at the melted plastic in disbelief.

"That shouldn't have happened," he said. "The equipment must be faulty."

"Your bloody brain is faulty!" Brian yelled, striding down the aisle towards him.

Kevin, the band's resident peacemaker stepped in front of him, shielding the bemused Colin.

"Cool it, Brian."

Brian brushed him aside. "I'm going to kill him."

"Wait!" Kevin put out a restraining hand. "At least wait till the gig's over. We need his van to get the gear back."

"If there is any gear worth saving," Brian said, between clenched teeth. "I'll just see if I can rescue it. If it's a write-off I am *definitely* going to kill him."

He couldn't decide which was the more desirable outcome. The pleasure of killing Colin might well outweigh the pain of losing the equipment.

Colin had been with the band for three weeks, ostensibly as rhythm guitar, but actually as unpaid roadie and driver. They kept him off the stage as much as possible and regularly failed to plug in his guitar. Recently, he had been getting on their nerves so much that even his willingness to buy rounds was not enough. Band morale was at an all-time low. He was going to have to go.

They had sacked him! The best player in the band! It was jealousy, that was what it was. It was him they cheered for at the end of the gig. The fans loved him. He was the best player and the best looking and the others couldn't take it. So they'd used the breakdown of their cheap equipment as an excuse. As if he would plug in the wrong plug. He knew what he was doing. He knew better than any of them. Just because Brian was an electrician he thought he knew more than he did. What a tosser! Well, he'd show them. He'd go solo.

"How did your jig go last night, Darling?"
"Gig, Mother."
Sylvia looked confused. She thought a gig was some kind of horse-drawn carriage.
Dennis looked up from his paper and watched his son guzzling a full English breakfast. The boy was already massively overweight but his mother insisted on feeding him as if he were a prize pig being groomed for a show.
He had difficulty believing Colin played in a band. He'd heard him play the guitar and couldn't imagine any band with a shred of self-esteem allowing him in.
"I was magnificent," Colin said. "The fans went wild. I'm seriously considering going solo".

Dennis sighed. Being in a boy band was just the latest of Colin's ephemeral (and mostly expensive) hobbies. So far he'd gone in for cycle racing (the memory of Colin in skin tight lycra still made him shudder), designing computer games (he'd failed to finish a single one), drama (the local amateur dramatic society had thrown him out after the first rehearsal – he had insisted he should play the romantic lead even though he weighed 16 stone, couldn't sing, couldn't remember his lines and had no experience). Dennis had drawn the line at motorbike scrambling (tempting, since there was a possibility he might kill himself) and joining a shooting club (for obvious reasons). What next?

Sylvia had spoilt him, of course, but you couldn't blame her. She'd had three miscarriages and a still-birth before the doctor had finally told her she should stop trying. They had left it too late. Her womb was already past its best when they finally got round to it. Maybe it had been sub-standard in the first place. Who knew?

She had been devastated -so distressed he was sure she was teetering on the edge of a nervous breakdown. And then the doctor had come up with the suggestion of adopting. He had another patient who was about to give birth to an unwanted child and he was sure he could organise a private adoption. Sylvia leapt at the chance.

Dennis was less sanguine. For a start, the doctor was a locum, standing in for their regular GP who was having some major surgery, and he was a little bit, well, odd. Dennis disliked him on sight. There was something robotic about him. His speech was too perfect, somehow and vaguely alien and he never blinked. He reminded him of a shop window dummy brought to life (but not in a good way). And did they do adoptions that way anymore? It was like something out of a Victorian novel. But he couldn't say no. It would have broken Sylvia's heart. Her last chance to have a child.

And, after all, there was no reason to suppose there was anything wrong with the baby. He seemed perfectly normal when he arrived. All his (many) character defects had probably been instilled by Sylvia, who had brought him up to believe he was the most wonderful human being who had ever walked the earth.

With a sinking feeling, Dennis returned to his paper.

~ * ~

Dennis had been dozing in his chair in front of the television when he was suddenly jerked into consciousness by the strident theme music of *Have I Got News for You*. Still befuddled with sleep, he watched as the panellists were introduced. Then he shot up in his seat and shouted, "Sylvia!"

"What?" Sylvia appeared at the door, drying a plate on a tea towel.

"Colin. It's our Colin. On the telly."

She looked at the screen, squinting a little. She really needed glasses these days but was too vain to wear them.

"That's Boris Johnson," she said. "I suppose he does look a bit like Colin, but not as handsome."

Printed in Great Britain
by Amazon

33771375R00149